Duffels

Edward Eggleston

Duffels

The present edition is a reproduction of previous publication of this classic work. Minor typographical errors may have been corrected without note; however, for an authentic reading experience the spelling, punctuation, and capitalization have been retained from the original text.

ISBN: 978-1-63637-376-8

CONTENTS

PREFACE

The once famous Mrs. Anne Grant—known in literature as Mrs. Grant of Laggan—spent part of her childhood in our New York Albany, then a town almost wholly given to traffic with the aborigines. To her we owe a description of the setting out of the young American-Dutch trader to ascend the Mohawk in a canoe, by laborious paddling and toilsome carrying round rifts and falls, in order to penetrate to the dangerous region of the tribes beyond the Six Nations. The outfit of this young "bushloper," as such a man was called in the still earlier Dutch period, consisted mainly of a sort of cloth suited to Indian wants. But there were added minor articles of use and fancy to please the youth or captivate the imagination of the women in the tribes. Combs, pocket mirrors, hatchets, knives, jew's-harps, pigments for painting the face blue, yellow, and vermilion, and other such things, were stored away in the canoe, to be spread out as temptations before the eyes of some group of savages rich in a winter's catch of furs. The cloths sold by the traders were called duffels, probably from the place of their origin, the town of Duffel, in the Low Countries. By degrees the word was, I suppose, transferred to the whole stock, and a trader's duffels included all the miscellany he carried with him. The romantic young bushloper, eager to accumulate money enough to marry the maiden he had selected, disappeared long ago from the water courses of northern New York. In his place an equally interesting figure—the Adirondack guide—navigates single-handed the rivers and lakes of the "North Woods." By one of those curious cases of transference that are often found in etymology, the guide still carries duffels, like his predecessor; but not for Indian trading. The word with him covers also an indefinite collection of objects of manifold use—camp utensils, guns, fishing tackle, and whatnots. The basket that sits in his light boat to hold his smaller articles is called a duffel basket, as was the basket of sundries in the trader's canoe, I fancy. If his camp grows into a house frequented

iv

by sportsmen, there will be a duffel room to contain all manner of unclassified things.

Like the trader of old New York, I here open my kit of duffels. I have selected from the shorter tales written by me since I began to deal in the fancy wares of a writer of fiction only such as seem to have elements of permanent interest. I find their range to be wide. They cover many phases of human nature; they describe life in both the eighteenth and the nineteenth centuries; they are of the East and of the West, of the North, the Middle, and the South. Group or classify them I can not; they are too various. Some were written long ago, in my younger manner, and in the tone prevailing among the story-writers of those days. Opinions and sentiments are inextricably interwoven with some of these earlier stories that do not seem to be mine to-day. But a man in his fifties ought to know how to be tolerant of the enthusiasms and beliefs of a younger man. I suspect that the sentiment I find somewhat foreign to me in the season of cooler pulses, and the situations and motives that seem rather naïve now, had something to do with the acceptability of the stories. The popularity of these early tales in their day encouraged me to go on, and a little later to set up in more permanent and wholesale business as a novelist. To certain of these stories of my apprenticeship I have appended dates to explain allusions in the text. Other stories there are here, that are of recent production, and by these I am willing to be judged. The variety in subject, manner, date, location, makes proper to them the title I have chosen—a good word with a savor of human history and an odor of the New World about it; a word yet in living use in this region of lakes and mountains. I am not without hope that some of my duffels will please.

If formal dedications were not a little old-fashioned, I should give myself the pleasure of writing on one of these pages the name of my friend Mr. Richard Watson Gilder. I have read with delight and sincere admiration the poems that have given him fame, but they need no praise of mine. The occasion of my mentioning his name here is more personal—it was by his solicitation that I was seduced, nearly a quarter of a century ago, into writing my earliest love story. I may say, perhaps without pushing the figure too far, that on his suggestion I first embarked in the light canoe of a dealer in duffels.

E. E.
Joshua's Rock, Lake George, 1893

SISTER TABEA

Two weather-beaten stone buildings at Ephrata, in Pennsylvania, remain as monuments on this side of the water of the great pietistic movement in Germany in the early part of the eighteenth century. One of these was called Bethany, the other Sharon. A hundred and thirty or forty years ago there were other buildings with these, and the softening hand of time had not yet touched any of them. The doorways were then, as now, on the ground level, the passages were just as narrow and dusky, the cells had the same little square windows to let in the day. But the stones in that day had a hue that reminded one of the quarry, the mortar between them was fresh, the shingles in the roof had gathered no moss and very little weather stain; the primeval forests were yet within the horizon, and there was everywhere an air of newness, of advancement, and of prosperity about the Dunkard Convent. One sees now neither monks nor nuns in these narrow hallways; monks and nuns are nowhere about Ephrata, except in the graveyard where all the brethren of Bethany, and all the sisters who once peopled Sharon, sleep together in the mold. But in the middle of the eighteenth century their bare feet shuffled upon the stairs as, clad in white hooded cloaks descending to the very ground, they glided in and out of the low doors, or assembled in the little chapel called "Zion" to attend service under the lead of their founder, Conrad Beissels. In the convent, where he reigned supreme, Beissels was known as Brother Friedsam; later he was reverently called Father Friedsam Gottrecht, a name that, like all their convent names, had plenty of mystical significance attached to it.

But monks and nuns are men and women; and neither cloister life, nor capuchin hoods and cloaks, nor bare feet, nor protracted midnight services, can prevent heartburnings and rivalries, nor can all of these together put down—what is most to be dreaded in a monastery—the growth of affection between man and woman. What could be done to tame human nature into submission, to bring it to rejoice only in unearthly meditations, and

1

a contented round of self-denial and psalm-singing, Brother Friedsam had tried on his followers with the unsparing hand of a religious enthusiast. He had forbidden all animal food. Not only was meat of evil tendency, but milk, he said, made the spirit heavy and narrow; butter and cheese produced similar disabilities; eggs excited the passions; honey made the eyes bright and the heart cheerful, but did not clear the voice for music. So he approved chiefly of those plain things that sprang direct from the earth, particularly of potatoes, turnips, and other roots, with a little bread soup and such like ghostly diet. For drink he would have nothing but what he called "innocent clear water," just as it flowed from the spring.

But even a dish of potatoes and turnips and beets and carrots, eaten from wooden trenchers, without milk or butter or meat, was not sufficient to make the affections and passions of men and women as ethereal as Friedsam wished. He wedded his people in mystic marriage to "the Chaste Lamb," to borrow his frequent phrase. They sang ecstatically of a mystical city of brotherly and sisterly affection which they, in common with other dreamers of the time, called Philadelphia, and they rejoiced in a divine creature called in their mystical jargon Sophia, which I suppose meant wisdom, wisdom divorced from common sense. These anchorites did not eschew social enjoyment, but held little love feasts. The sisters now invited the brethren, and next the brethren entertained the sisters—with unbuttered parsnips and draughts of innocent clear water, no doubt.

That which was most remarkable at Ephrata, and that out of which grows my story, was the music. Brother Friedsam, besides his cares of organization, finance, and administration, and his mystical theological speculations, was also a poet. Most of the songs sung in the little building called "Zion" were written by him—songs about "the lonesome turtledove in the wilderness," that is, the Church; songs in praise of the mystical marriage of virgins with the chaste Lamb; songs about the Philadelphian brotherhood of saints, about the divine Sophia, and about many other things which no man can understand, I am sure, until he has first purified himself

2

from the gross humors of the flesh by a heavenly diet of turnips and spring water. To the brethren and sisters who believed their little community in the Pennsylvania woods to be "the Woman in the Wilderness" seen by St. John, these words represented the only substantial and valuable things in the wide universe; and they sang the songs of Conrad Beissels with as much fervor as they could have sung the songs of heaven itself. Beissels—the Friedsam of the brotherhood—was not only the poet but the composer of the choral songs, and a composer of rare merit. The music he wrote is preserved as it was copied out with great painstaking by the brethren and sisters. In looking over the wonderful old manuscript notebook, the first impression is one of delight with the quaint symbolic illuminations wrought by the nuns of Ephrata upon the margins. But those who know music declare that the melodies are lovely, and that the whole structure of the harmonies is masterful, and worthy of the fame they had in the days when monks and nuns performed them under the lead of Brother Friedsam himself. In the gallery of Zion house, but concealed from the view of the brethren, sat the sisterhood, like a company of saints in spotless robes. Below, the brethren, likewise in white, answered to the choir above in antiphonal singing of the loveliest and most faultless sort. Strangers journeyed from afar over rough country roads to hear this wonderful chorus, and were moved in the depths of their souls with the indescribable sweetness and loftiness of the music, and with the charm and expressiveness of its rendering by these pale-faced other-worldly singers.

But their perfection of execution was attained at a cost almost too great. Brother Friedsam was a fanatic, and he was also an artist. He obliged the brethren and sisters to submit to the most rigorous training. In this, as in religion, he subordinated them to his ideals. He would fain tune their very souls to his own key; and he exacted a precision that was difficult of attainment by men and women of average fallibility and carelessness. The men singers were divided into five choruses of five persons each; the sisters were classified, according to the pitch of their voices, into three divisions, each of which sang or kept silent, according to the duty assigned to it in the notebook. At the love-feasts these choruses sat side by side at the table, so as to be ready to sing together with perfect precision whenever a song should be announced. At the singing school Brother Friedsam could not abide the least defect; he rated roundly the brother or sister who made any mistake; he scourged their lagging aspirations toward perfection. If it is ever necessary to account for bad temper in musicians, one might suggest that the water-gruel diet had impaired his temper and theirs; certain it is that out of the production of so much heavenly harmony there sprang discord. The brethren and sisters grew daily more and more indignant at the severity of the director, whom they reverenced as a religious guide, but against whom, as a musical conductor, they rebelled in their hearts.

The sisters were the first to act in this crisis. At their knitting and their sewing they talked about it, in the kitchen they discussed it, until their hearts burned within them. Even in illuminating the notebook with pretty billing turtledoves, and emblematic flowers such as must have grown in paradise, since nothing of the sort was ever known in any earthly garden—even in painting these, some of the nuns came near to spoiling their colors and blurring their pages with tears.

Only Margaretha Thome, who was known in the convent as Sister Tabea, shed no tears. She worked with pen and brush, and heard the others talk; now and then, when some severe word of Brother Friedsam's was repeated, she would look up with a significant flash of the eye.

"The Hofcavalier doesn't talk," said Sister Thecla. This Thecla had given the nickname of "Hofcavalier" (noble courtier), to Tabea at her first arrival in the convent on account of her magnificent figure and high carriage.

"You shouldn't give nicknames, Sister Thecla."

The last speaker was a sister with an austere face and gray eyes which had no end of cold-blooded religious enthusiasm in them.

"I need not give you a nickname," retorted Thecla to the last speaker; "Brother Friedsam did that when he called you Jael. You are just the kind of person to drive a tent-nail through a man's head."

"If he were the enemy of the Church of God," said Jael, in a voice as hard as it was sincere.

Then the talk drifted back to the singing school and Brother Friedsam's severity.

"But why doesn't the Hofcavalier speak?" again persisted Thecla.

"When the Hofcavalier speaks, it will be to Brother Friedsam himself," answered Tabea.

The temerity of this proposition took Thecla's breath, but it set the storm a-going more vigorously than before among the sisterhood, who, having found somebody ready to bell the cat, grew eager to have the cat belled. Only Sister Jael, who for lack of voice was not included in either of the three choruses of the sisterhood, stoutly defended Brother Friedsam, thinking, perhaps, that it was not a bad thing to have the conceit of the singers reduced; indeed, she was especially pleased that Tabea, the unsurpassed singer of the sisters' gallery, should have suffered rebuke.

At length it was agreed that Tabea should tell Brother Friedsam that the sisters did not intend to go to singing school again.

Then Tabea lifted up her dark head and regarded the circle of women in white garments about her.

"You are all brave now, but when Brother Friedsam shakes his finger at you, you will every one of you submit as though you were a set of redemptioners bought with his money. When I tell Brother Friedsam that I shall not come to singing school, I shall stick to it. He may get his music performed by some one else. He will not call me a 'ninny' again."

"There spoke the Hofcavalier," giggled Thecla.

"Sister Tabea," said Jael, "if you go on as you are going, you will end by leaving the convent and breaking your vows. Mark my words."

"I am going to finish this turtledove first, though," said Tabea gayly.

It was finally agreed that if Tabea would speak to the director on behalf of the sisterhood, the sisters would resolutely stand by their threat, and that they would absent themselves from Brother Friedsam's music drills long enough to have him understand that they were not to be treated like children. To the surprise of all, Tabea left her work at once, covered up her head with the hood attached to her gown, and sought the lodge of Brother Friedsam, which stood between Bethany and Sharon.

When Tabea was admitted to the cell, and stood before the revered Friedsam, she felt an unexpected palpitation. Nor was Beissels any more composed. He could never speak to this girl without some mental disturbance.

"Brother Friedsam," she said, "I am sent by the sisters to say that they are very indignant at your treatment of them in the rehearsals, and that they are not going to attend them hereafter."

Beissels's sensitive lips quivered a moment; this sudden rebellion surprised him, and he did not at first see how to meet it.

"You suggested this course to them, I suppose?" he said after a pause.

"No, Brother Friedsam, I had nothing to do with it until now. But I think they are right, and I hope they will keep to their word. You have been altogether too hard on us."

The director made no reply, but wearily leaned his pale, refined face upon his hand and looked up at Tabea. This look of inquiry had something of unhappiness in it that touched the nun's heart, and she was half sorry that she had spoken so sharply. She fumbled for the wooden latch of the door presently, and went out with a sense of inward defeat and annoyance.

"The Hofcavalier does not come back with head in the air," murmured Thecla. "A bad sign."

"I gave the message," said Sister Tabea, "and Brother Friedsam did not say whether the four parts sung by the men would be sufficient or not. But I know very well what he will do; he will coax you all back within a week."

"And you will leave the convent and break your vows; mark my words," said Sister Jael with sharpness.

6

"It will be after I get this page finished, I tell you," said Tabea. But she did not seem in haste to finish the page, for, not choosing to show how much she had been discomposed by Brother Friedsam's wistful and inquiring look, she gathered up her brush, her colors, and the notebook page on which she had been at work, and went up the stairs alongside the great chimney, shutting herself in her cell.

Once there, the picture of Friedsam's face came vividly before her. She recalled her first meeting with him at her mother's house on the Wissahickon, and how her heart had gone out to the only man she had ever met whose character was out of the common. I do not say that she had consciously loved him as she listened to him, sitting there on the homemade stool in her mother's cabin and talking of things beyond comprehension. But she could have loved him, and she did worship him. It was the personal fascination of Brother Friedsam and her own vigorous hatred of the commonplace that had led her three years before to join the sisterhood in the Sharon house. She did not know to what degree a desire for Beissels's companionship had drawn her to accept his speculations concerning the mystical Sophia and the Philadelphian fellowship. But the convent had proved a disappointment. She had seen little of the great Brother Friedsam, and he had given her, instead of friendly notice and approval, only a schoolmaster's scolding now and then for slight faults committed in singing a new piece.

As she sat there in gloomy meditation Jael's evil prediction entered her mind, and she amused herself with dreams of what might take place if she should leave the convent and go out into the world again.

In putting away her papers a little note fell out.

"The goose is at it again," she said.

She had that day received some blank paper from the paper mill of the community, and Daniel Scheible had put this little love letter into the package of which he was the bearer. He had sent such letters before, and Tabea, though she had not answered them, had kept them, partly because she did not wish to inform those in authority of this breach of rule, partly because so much defiance of the law of the place gave a little zest to a monotonous life, and partly because she was a young woman, and therefore not displeased with affection, even from a youth in whom she had no more than a friendly interest.

Scheible's parents had been Dunkards, persecuted in Europe, who had sought refuge from their troubles by the bad expedient of taking ship for Philadelphia, with an understanding that they were, according to custom, to be sold for a term of years to pay the fare. Among a multitude who died on the passage from the overcrowding and bad food were Daniel's father and mother, and the little lad was sold for the rest of his minority to pay his own fare as well as that of the dead members of his family. As a promising boy, he had been bought by the Ephrata brotherhood and bred into the fraternity. With the audacity of youth he had conceived a great passion for Tabea, and now that his apprenticeship was about to expire he amused her with surreptitious notes. To-day, for the first time, Tabea began to think of the possibility of marrying Scheible, chiefly, perhaps, from a vague desire to escape from the convent, which could not but be irksome to one of her spirit. Scheible was ambitious, and it was his plan, as she knew, to go to Philadelphia to make his fortune; and she and he together, what might they not do? Then she laughed at herself for such a day dream, and went out to do her share of household duties, singing mellifluously, as she trod barefoot through the passages, a mystic song of hope and renunciation:

"Welt, packe dich;
Ich sehne mich
Nur nach dem Himmel.
Denn droben ist Lachen und Lieben und Leben;
Hier unten ist Alles dem Eiteln ergeben."

Which rendered may read:

"World, get you gone;
I strive alone
To attain heaven.
There above is laughter, life, and love;
Here below one must all vanity forego."

But though to-day she sang of the laughter that is above, she was less unworldly on the morrow. Brother Friedsam, as she had foreseen, began to break down the rebellion about the singing school. He was too good a strategist to attack the strong point of the insurrection first. He began with good-natured Thecla, who could laugh away yesterday's vexations, and so one by one he conquered the opposition in detail. He shrank from assailing the Hofcavalier until he should have won the others, knowing well the obstinacy of her resolution. And when all the rest had yielded he still said nothing to Tabea, either because he deemed it of no use, or because he thought neglect might do her rebellious spirit good. But if this last were his plan, he had miscalculated the vigor of her determination.

"Do you know," said the good-hearted, gossipy little Sister Persida, coming into Tabea's cell two or three days later, "that the sisters have all yielded to Brother Friedsam? He coaxed and managed them so, you know. Has he talked to you?"

"No."

"You'll have to give up when he does. Nobody can resist Brother Friedsam."

"I can."

"You always scare me so, Sister Tabea; I wouldn't dare hold up my head as you do."

But when Persida had gone out the high head of the Hofcavalier went down a little. She felt that the man whom she in some sort worshiped had put upon her a public slight. He did not account it worth his while to invite her to return. She had missed her chance to refuse. Just what connection Brother Friedsam's slight had with Daniel Scheible's love letters I leave the reader to determine. But in her anger she fished these notes out of a basket

9

used to hold her changes of white raiment, and read them all over slowly, line by line, and for the first time with a lively interest in their contents. They were very ingenious; and they very cleverly pictured to her the joys of a home of her own with a devoted husband. She found evidences of very amiable traits in the writer. But why should I trace in detail the curious but familiar process by which a girl endows a man with all the qualities she wishes him to possess?

The very next day Scheible, who had been melancholy ever since he began to send to Tabea letters that brought no answer, was observed to be in a mood so gleeful that his companions in the paper mill doubted his sanity. The fountain of this joy was a note from Tabea stowed away in the pocket of his gown. She had not signed it with her convent title, but with the initials M. T., for her proper name, Margaretha Thome. There were many fluctuations in Tabea's mind and many persuasive notes from Scheible before the nun at length promised to forsake the convent, now grown bitter to her, for the joys of a home. Even then Daniel could not help feeling insecure in regard to a piece of good fortune so dazzling, and he sent note after note to urge her to have the day for the wedding fixed.

Meantime the young man created but little sensation by leaving the mill, as his term of apprenticeship had expired, and he had never professed much attachment to the brotherhood.

Sister Tabea had persistently omitted the rehearsals, and so the grand chorals were now given on the Sabbaths without her voice, and Jael felt no little exultation at this state of things. At length, after much wavering, Tabea made a final resolution to leave the convent, and to accept the love of the adventurous youth who had shown so persistent an affection for her.

As soon as the day of the wedding was arranged by means of the surreptitious notes which she continued to exchange with Scheible, she prepared to leave Sharon and Ephrata. But nothing could be farther from her plans than the project proposed by her lover that she should elope with him at night. Tabea meant to march out with all her colors flying.

10

First of all she went to see the sinister prophetess, Sister Jael.

"I've finished that turtledove, Sister Jael, and now I am going to leave the sisterhood and marry Daniel Scheible."

Nothing is so surprising to a prophet as the fulfillment of his most confident prediction. Jael looked all aghast, and her face splintered into the most contradictory lines in the effort to give expression to the most conflicting emotions.

"I'm astonished at you," she said reprovingly, when she got breath.

"Why, I thought you expected it," replied Tabea.

"Will you break your vow?"

"Yes. Why shouldn't a woman break a vow made by a girl? And so, good-by, Sister Jael. Can't you wish me much joy?"

But Jael turned sharply away in a horror that could find no utterance.

Thecla laughed, as was her wont, and wished Tabea happiness, but intimated that Daniel was a bold man to undertake to subdue the Hofcavalier. Sister Persida's woman's heart was set all a-flutter, and she quite forgot that she was trying to be a nun, and that she belonged to the solitary and forsaken turtledove in the wilderness. She whispered in Tabea's ear: "You'll look so nice when you're married, dear, and Daniel will be so pleased, and the young men will steal your slipper off your foot at the dinner table, and how I wish I could be there to see you married! But oh, Tabea! I don't see how you dare to face them all! I'd just run away with all my might if I were in your place."

And so each one took the startling intelligence according to her character, and soon all work was suspended, and every inmate of Sharon was gathered in unwonted excitement in the halls and the common room.

When Tabea passed out of the low-barred door of Sharon she met the radiant face of Scheible, who had tied his two saddle horses a little way off.

"Come quickly, Tabea," he said with impatience.

"No, Daniel; it won't do to be rude. I must tell Brother Friedsam good-by."

11

"No, don't," said Daniel, turning pale with terror. "If you go in to see the director you will never come with me."

"Why won't I?" laughed the defiant girl.

"He's a wizard, and has charms that he gets out of his great books. Don't go in there; you'll never get away."

Daniel held to the Pennsylvania Dutch superstitions, but Tabea only laughed, and said, "I am not afraid of wizards." She looked the Hofcavalier more than ever as she left the trembling fellow and went up to the door of Brother Friedsam's lodge.

"She isn't afraid of the devil," muttered Scheible.

Tabea knocked at the door.

"Come in and welcome, whoever thou art," said the director within.

But when she had lifted the latch and pushed back the door, squeaking on its wooden hinges, Tabea found that Friedsam was engaged in some business with the prior of the convent, the learned Dr. Peter Miller, known at Ephrata as Brother Jabez. Friedsam did not at first look up. The delay embarrassed her; she had time to see, with painful clearness, all the little articles in the slenderly furnished room. She noticed that the billet of wood which lay for a pillow, according to the Ephrata custom, on a bare bench used for a bed, was worn upon one side with long use; she saw how the bell rope by means of which Friedsam called the brethren and sisters to prayers at any hour in the night, hung dangling near the bench, so that the bell might be pulled on a sudden inspiration even while the director was rising from his wooden couch; she noted the big books; and then a great reverence for his piety and learning fell upon her, and a homesick regret; and Scheible and the wedding frolic did not seem so attractive after all. Nevertheless she held up her head like a defiant Hofcavalier.

After a time Brother Jabez, with a kind greeting, passed her, and the director, looking up, said very gently:

"I wish you a very good day, Sister Tabea."

"I am no longer Sister Tabea, but Margaretha Thome. I have said adieu to all in Sharon, and now I come to say good-by to Brother Friedsam. I am going to lay aside these garments and marry Daniel Scheible."

12

She held out her hand, but Friedsam was too much stunned to see it.

"You have broken your vow! You have denied the Lord!"

There was no severity in his despondent rebuke; it had the vibration of an involuntary cry of surprise and pain.

Tabea was not prepared for this. Severity she could have defied; but this cry of a prophet awakened her own conscience, and she trembled as if she had been in the light of a clear-seeing divine judgment.

"You can speak so, Brother Friedsam, for you have no human weaknesses. I am not suited to a convent; I never can be happy here. I am not submissive. I want to be necessary to somebody. Nobody cares for me here. You do not mind whether I sing in the chorals or not, and you will be better pleased to have me away, and I am going." Then, finding that the director remained silent, she said, with emotion: "Brother Friedsam, I have a great reverence for you, but I wish you knew something of the infirmities of a heart that wants to love and to be loved by somebody, and then maybe you would not think so very hardly of Tabea after she has gone."

There was a tone of beseeching in these last words which Tabea had not been wont to use.

The director looked more numb now than ever. Tabea's words had given him a rude blow, and he could not at once recover. His lips moved without speaking, and his face assumed a look betokening inward suffering.

"Great God of wisdom, must I then tell her?" said Friedsam when he got breath. He stood up and gazed out of the square window in indecision.

"Tabea," he said presently, turning full upon her and looking into her now pale face upturned to the light, "I thought my secret would die in my breast, but you wring it from me. You say that I have no infirmities—no desire for companionship like other men or women. It is the voice of Sophia, the wisdom of the Almighty, that bids me humble myself before you this day."

Here he paused in visible but suppressed emotion. "These things," he said, pointing to his wooden couch, "these hardships of the body, these self-denials of my vocation, give me no trouble. I have one great soul-affliction, and that is what you reproach me for lacking, namely, the longing to love and to be loved. And that trial you laid upon me the first time I saw your face and heard your words in your mother's house on the Wissahickon. O Tabea, you are not like the rest! you are not like the rest! Even when you go wrong, it is not like the rest. It is the vision of the life I might have led with such a woman as you that troubles my dreams in the night-time, when, across the impassable gulf of my irrevocable vow, I have stretched out my hands in entreaty to you."

This declaration changed instantly the color of Tabea's thoughts of life. Daniel Scheible and his little love scrawls seemed to her lofty spirit as nothing now that she saw herself in the light thrown upon her by the love of the great master whose spirit had evoked Ephrata, and whose genius uttered itself in angelic harmonies. She loathed the little life that now opened before her. There seemed nothing in heaven or earth so desirable as to possess the esteem of Friedsam. But she stood silent and condemned.

"I have had one comfort," proceeded Brother Friedsam after a while. "When I have perceived your strength of character, when I have heard your exquisite voice uttering the melodies with which I am inspired, I have thought my work was sweeter because Tabea shared it, and I have hoped that you would yet more and more share it as years and discipline should ripen your spirit."

The director felt faint; he sat down and looked dejectedly into the corner of the room farthest away from where Tabea stood. He roused himself in a few moments, and turned about again, to find Tabea kneeling on the flagstones before him.

"I have denied the Lord!" she moaned, for her judgment had now come completely round to Friedsam's standpoint. His condemnation seemed bitterer than death. "Brother Friedsam, I have denied the Lord!"

Friedsam regarded the kneeling figure for a moment, and then he reached out his hands, solemnly placing them on her head with a motherly tenderness, while a tremor went through his frame.

"Thou, dear child, shalt do thy first work over again," he said.

14

"Thou shalt take a new vow, and when thou art converted then shalt thou, like Peter, strengthen the others." And, withdrawing his hands, he said: "I will pray for you, Tabea, every night of my life when I hear the cock crow."

Tabea rose up slowly and went out at the door, walking no longer like a Hofcavalier, but like one in a trance. Dimly she saw the sisters standing without the door of Sharon; there was Thecla, with half-amused face, and there was Persida, curious as ever; there were Sister Petronella and Sister Blandina and others, and behind all the straight, tall form of austere Jael. Without turning to the right or to the left, Tabea directed her steps to the group at the door of Sharon.

"No! no! come, dear Tabea!" It was the voice of Daniel Scheible, whose existence she had almost forgotten.

"Poor Daniel!" she said, pausing and looking at him with pity.

"Don't say 'Poor Daniel,' but come."

"Poor boy!" said Tabea.

"You are bewitched!" he cried, seizing her and drawing her away. "I knew Friedsam would put a charm on you."

She absently allowed him to lead her a few steps; then, with another look full of tender pity and regret at his agitated face, she extricated herself from his embrace and walked rapidly to the door. Quickening her steps to escape his pursuing grasp, she pushed through the group of sisters and fled along the hallway and up the stairs, closing the door of her cell and fastening down the latch.

Scheible, sure that she was under some evil spell, rushed after her, shook himself loose from the grip of Sister Jael, who sought to stop him, and reached the door of Tabea's cell. But all his knocking brought not one word of answer, and after a while Brother Jabez came in and led the poor fellow out, to the great grief of Sister Persida, who in her heart thought it a pity to spoil a wedding.

The sisters who came to call Tabea to supper that evening also failed to elicit any response. Late in the night, when she had become calm, Tabea heard the crowing of a cock, and her heart was deeply touched at the thought that Friedsam, the revered Friedsam, now more than ever the beloved of her soul, was at that moment going to prayer for the disciple who had broken her vow. She rose from her bench and fell on her knees; and if she mistook the mingled feelings of penitence and human passion for pure devotion, she made the commonest mistake of enthusiastic spirits.

But she was not left long to doubt that Friedsam had remembered her; by the time that the cock had crowed the second time the sound of the monastery bell, the rope of which hung just by Friedsam's bedside, broke abruptly into the deathlike stillness, calling the monks and nuns of Ephrata to a solemn night service. Tabea felt sure that Friedsam had called the meeting at this moment by way of assuring her of his remembrance.

Daniel Scheible, who had wandered back to the neighborhood in the aimlessness of disappointment, heard the monastery bell waking all the reverberations of the forest, and saw light after light twinkle from the little square windows of Bethany and Sharon; then he saw the monks and nuns come out of Bethany and Sharon, each carrying a small paper lantern as they hastened to Zion. The bell ceased, and Zion, which before had been wrapped in night, shone with light from every window, and there rose upon the silence the voices of the choruses chanting an antiphonal song; and disconsolate Scheible cursed Friedsam and Ephrata, and went off into outer darkness.

When the first strophe had been sung below, and the sweet-voiced sisters caught up the antistrophe, Brother Friedsam, sitting in the midst, listened with painful attention, vainly trying to detect the sound of Tabea's voice. But when the second strophe had been sung, and the sisters began their second response, a thrill of excitement went through all as the long-silent voice of Sister Tabea rose above the rest with even more than its old fervor and expression.

And the next Saturday—for the seventh day was the Ephrata Sabbath—Tabea took a new, solemn, and irrevocable vow; and from that time until the day of her death she was called Sister Anastasia—the name signifying that she had been re-established. What source of consolation Anastasia had the rest never divined. How should they guess that alongside her religious fervor a human love grew ethereally like an air plant?

16

Note.—Much of this little story is fact. I have supplied details, dialogue, and passion. For the facts which constitute the groundwork I am chiefly indebted to Dr. Oswald W. Seidensticker's very valuable monograph entitled "Ephrata, eine amerikanische Klostergeschichte." The reader will find a briefer account of the monastery from the same learned and able writer in The Century magazine for December, 1881.

THE REDEMPTIONER

A STORY IN THREE SCENES

PROLOGUE

The stories we write are most of them love stories; but in the lives of men there are also many stories that are not love stories: some, truly, that are hate stories. The main incident of the one I am about to tell I found floating down from the eighteenth century on the stream of Maryland tradition. It serves to present some of our forefathers, not as they seem in patriotic orations and reverent family traditions, but as they appear to a student of the writings and prints of their own age.

SCENE I

The time was a warm autumn day in the year 1751. The place was a plantation on the Maryland shore of the Potomac. A planter of about thirty years of age, clad in buckskin shortclothes, sat smoking his pipe, after his noonday meal, in the wide entry that ran through his double log house from the south side to the north, the house being of the sort called alliteratively "two pens and a passage." The planter's wife sat over against him, on the other side of the passage, carding home-grown cotton wool with hand cards. He had placed his shuck-bottom chair so as to see down the long reach to the eastward, where the widening Potomac spread itself between low-lying banks, with never a brown hill to break the low horizon line. Every now and again he took his cob pipe from his mouth, and scanned the distant water wistfully.

"I know what you're looking for, Mr. Browne," said his wife, as she reversed her hand cards and rubbed the carded cotton between the smooth backs of the two implements to make it into a roll for spinning. "You're looking to see the Nancy Jane come sailing into the river one of these days."

"That's just what I'm looking after," he answered.

"Why should you care?" she said. "You don't expect her to fetch you a new bonnet and a hoop skirt seven feet wide." She laughed merrily at her own speech, which, after all, was but a trifling exaggeration of the width of a hoop skirt in that time.

Sanford Browne did not laugh, but took his pipe from his mouth, and stood up a moment, straining his sight once more against the distant horizon, where the green-blue water of the wide estuary melted into the blue-green of the sky with hardly a line of demarcation. Then he sat down and took a dry tobacco leaf lying on a stool beside him and crushed it to powder by first chafing it between his open hands and then grinding it in the palm of his left hand, rubbing it with the thumb of his right in a mortar-and-pestle fashion.

"I've a good deal more reason to look for the Nancy Jane than you have, Judy. I wrote my factor, you know, to find some trace of my father and mother, or of my sister Susan, if it took the half of my tobacco crop. I hope he'll find them this time." Saying this, he filled his cob pipe with the powdered tobacco, and then rose and walked into the large western room of the house, which served for kitchen and dining-room. It was also the weaving-room, and the great heavy-beamed loom stood in the corner. At the farther end was the vast, smoke-blackened stone fireplace, with two large rude andirons and a swinging crane. A skillet and a gridiron stood against the jamb on one side, a hoe for baking hoe cakes and a little wrought-iron trivet were in order on the other. The breakfast fire had burned out; only the great backlog, hoary with gray ashes, lay slumbering at the back of the fireplace. The planter poked the drift of ashes between the andirons with a green oak stick until he saw a live coal shining red in the gray about it. This he rolled out upon the hearth, and then took it between thumb and finger and deposited it within the bowl of his pipe by a deft motion, which gave it no time to burn him.

19

Having got his pipe a-going, he strolled back into the wide passage and scanned the horizon once more. Judith Browne did not like to see her husband in this mood. She knew well how vain every exercise of her wifely arts of diversion would prove when he once fell into this train of black thoughts; but she could not refrain from essaying the hopeless task by holding up her apron of homespun cloth full of cotton rolls, pretty in their whiteness and roundness and softness, meantime coquettishly turning her still girlish head on one side, and saying: "Now, Mr. Browne, why don't you praise my cotton? Did you ever see better carding than that?"

The young planter took a roll of the cotton in his hands, holding it gingerly, and essaying absentmindedly to yield to his wife's mood. Just at that moment Sanford Browne the younger, a boy about eight years of age, came round the corner of the house and stood in front of his father, with his feet wide apart, feeling among the miscellanies in the bottom of his pocket for a periwinkle shell.

"How would you like to have him spirited away by a crimp, Judy?" demanded the husband, replacing the cotton and pointing to the lad.

"I should just die, dear," said Judy Browne in a low voice.

"That's what happened to my mother, I suppose," said Browne. "I hope she died; it would be too bad to think that she had to live all these twenty-two years imagining all sorts of things about her lost little boy. I remember her, Judy, the day I saw her last. I went out of a side street into Fleet Street, and then I grew curious and went on out through Temple Bar into the road they call the Strand. I did not know how far I had gone from the city until I heard the great bell of St. Martin's in the Fields chiming at five o'clock. I turned toward the city again, but stopped along the way to look at the noblemen's houses. Somehow, at last I got into Lincoln's Inn Fields and could not tell which way to go. Just then a sea captain came up to me, and, pretending to know me, told me he would fetch me to my father. I went with him, and he got me into a boat and so down to his ship below the bridge. The ship was already taking aboard a lot of kids and freewillers out of the cook

20

houses, where some of them had been shut up for weeks. I cried and begged for my father, but the captain only kicked and cuffed me. It was a long and wretched voyage, as I have told you often. I was brought here and sold to work with negroes and convicts. I don't so much mind the beatings I got, or the hard living, but to think of all my mother has suffered, and that I shall never see her or my father again! If I ever lay eyes on that Captain Lewis, he will go to the devil before he has time to say any prayers."

"I'd like to shoot him," said the boy, in sympathy with his father's mood. "I'll kill him when I get big enough, pappy." And he went off to seek the bow and arrow given him by an Indian who lingered in the region once occupied by his tribe.

"Never mind," said the wife, stroking her husband's arm, "you are getting rich now, and your hard times are over."

"Yes, but everybody will always remember that I was a bought redemptioner, and your folks will hardly ever forgive you for marrying me."

"Oh, yes, they will some day. If you keep on as lucky as you are, I shall live in a bigger house than any of them, and drive to church behind six horses. That'll make a great difference. If the Nancy Jane fetches me a London bonnet and a wide, wide petticoat such as the Princess Augusta wears, so that I can brush against the pews on both sides with my silk frock when I go down the aisle, my folks will already begin to think that Sanford Browne is somebody," and she made little motions of vanity as she fancied her entrance into Duck Creek parish church on the Sunday after the arrival of the tobacco ship, arrayed in imitation of the Princess of Wales, the news of whose recent widowhood had not yet reached Judy Browne.

"There comes the Nancy Jane now," called the boy from the dooryard, pointing to a sloop on the other side of the wide estuary, bowling in with topsail and jib furled, and her rusty mainsail bellying under pressure of a wind dead aft.

"That's not the Nancy Jane," said the father; "only a sloop. But I don't know whose. Oh, yes; it must be that Yankee peddler back again. There's his codfish ensign at his masthead. He's making for the other side now, but he'll come over here to sell his rum and kickshaws before he goes out."

21

"Hello, Mr. Browne!" It was a voice coming from the river in front of the house. The owner of the voice was concealed by some bushes at the margin of the water.

"Hello!" answered Browne to the invisible caller. "Is that you, Mr. Wickford?"

"I've got some letters for you, Mr. Browne," came back from the water. "The Nancy Jane ran in on the east wind this morning before daylight, and anchored in the little oyster bay below Manley's. She brings news that the Prince of Wales died last Spring. I happened to come past there this morning, and I brought some things Captain Jackson had for you. I reckon there's something pretty here for Mrs. Browne, too. Send one of your boys down."

"I'll come myself," said Browne, going down the bank, followed eagerly by the little Sanford, who had also his interest in the arrival of the parcels from London. There came after them presently a lithe young negro boy of fifteen, not yet two years out of Africa. He was clad in nothing but his native blackness, which was deemed sufficient for a half-grown negro in that day. Mrs. Browne had sent black Jocko after the others with orders to bring up her things "without waiting for the gentlemen to get done talking."

But the gentlemen did not talk very long. The neighbor was desirous of getting on to have the first telling of the news about the death of Prince Frederick, and Mr. Browne was impatient to open the packet from his factor.

"Good-by, Mr. Wickford. Come down and see us some time, and bring all your family," he called as the neighbor's canoe shot away in answer to the lusty paddle strokes of his men.

"I reckon we'll come, sir," answered the receding neighbor. "My wife'll want to see what Mrs. Browne got from London. Tell Mrs. Browne we're afraid she'll be too fine to know her neighbors when she puts on her new bonnet."

The last words of this neighborly chaff were shouted over a wide sheet of water, and Sanford Browne, halfway up the bank, made no reply, but went back to his chair in the passage and opened his packet. Kid that he had been, Browne had contrived to learn to read and write from a convict bought for a schoolmaster by

22

the planter to whom Browne had been sold. This lettered rogue took pity on the kidnaped child, and gave him lessons on nights and Sunday, because he was well born and not willing to sink to the condition of the servants about him.

Browne found his factor's letter occupied at the outset with an account of the tobacco market and congratulations on the high price obtained for the last year's crop. Then the factor proceeded to give a bill of sales, and then a list of things purchased for Browne and his family, with the price set down for the hoop skirt and the new bonnet and the silk frock, as well as for a cocked hat and dress periwig necessary to Sanford Browne's increasing dignity, and some things for the little Sanford. Browne studied each successive page of the letter in hope of finding a word on the subject in which he was most deeply interested, stopping reluctantly now and then to look up when his wife would break in with:

"Mr. Browne! Mr. Browne! won't you just look this way a minute? Isn't this fine?"

"Yes, Judy; it surely is," he would say absently, keeping his thumb on the place in the factor's letter, and resuming his reading as soon as possible, without having any definite idea of what Mrs. Judith had been showing him.

On the very last page he found these words:

"I have made most diligent searche for your family as you required butt I have not discovered muche that will be to your satisfaction. I send you, Sir, a coppie of certain things sette down in the Parish Register of St. Clement Danes, wch I thoughte most like to be of interest to you. Bye these you will discover that Walter Sanford Browne was born the 27 daye of the moneth of Febuarie 1721—wch will no doubt give you exacte knowledge of your owne age. The father and mother of Walter Sanford Browne bore the names Walter and Susan respectively wch is a fact that will not be indifferent to you I suppose. I finde that Walter Browne aforesd, who is sette down a scrivener, was married at this same church of St. Clements on the 22 daye

23

of Marche in the year 1720 to Anne Sanford of the same parish. Theire daughter Susan was borne in Aprill 1725, as you will see by this transcripte made by the clarke of the parish. The clarke cannot discover any further mencion of this familie nor of the name of Sanford in this register downe to this present time, from wch he deems it is to be inferred that sd. Walter Browne long since removed out of that parish, in particular as the present wardens and sidesmen of the parish afresd do not know any man of that name now residente there. It is a probabilitie that yr. father has removed to one of the plantations. I have made public advertisement in the Gazettes for your father or any neare kinsman but w'out any successe whatsoever."

There followed a memorandum of pounds, shillings, and pence paid to the "clarke" of the parish of St. Clement Danes, of money paid for advertisements in the gazettes, and of expenses incurred in further searches made by a solicitor. That was all—the end of hope to Sanford Browne. He went into the sitting-room and put the factor's letter into a little clothespress that stood beside the chimney, and then strode out into the air, giving no heed to Judith, who had gone up the stairs at the side of the passage, and come down again wearing a hideous pannier petticoat under her new frock. She guessed her husband's disappointment, and, though she longed for a word of admiration, or at least of wondering attention, for her square-rigged petticoat, she thought best to be content with the excited prattle of her maid, a young bond-servant bought off the Nancy Jane the year before.

"Here, Jocko," said Browne, standing in front of his house and calling to the Adamite negro lad, "you go and call Bob, and get the sloop ready. I'm going down to the ship."

"Get sloop, massa?" said the negro, speaking English with difficulty. "Massa say sloop?"

Sanford Browne looked at the black figure inquiringly. It was not often that poor, cringing Jocko ventured to question him. "Yes, sloop," he said with an emphasis born of his irritating disappointment.

24

"Much great big wind blow—blow right up river. Tack, tack, all day," muttered the black boy timidly.

"You're right," said the planter, who had not observed that the strong wind would be dead ahead all the way to the anchorage. "Tell Bob to put the canoe in the water." And then to himself: "The negro is no fool."

"Bob, Bob, massa him want can-noo go see great big ship mighty quick."

"Come, Sanford; you may go too," said the planter to his son. "We'll carry the fowling piece: there'll be ducks on the water."

SCENE II

The time is the same day, and the place the deck of the Nancy Jane, at anchor. The captain is giving orders to the cook: "I want a good bowl of bumbo set here on deck against the planters come aboard." Then turning to the mate: "Have the decks squeegeed clean, an' everything shipshape. Put the rogues in as good garb as you can. You'll find a few wigs in a box in my cabin. But these on the likeliest, and make 'em say they're mechanics, or merchants' clerks, and housemaids. Tell 'em if they don't put out a good foot and get off our hands soon we'll tie 'em up and make 'em understand that it's better to lie to a planter than to stick on shipboard too long. Make the women clean themselves up and look tidy like ancient housemaids, and don't allow any nonsense. Tell 'em if they swear or quarrel while the planters are aboard they'll get a cat-o'-nine-tails well laid on. We've got to make 'em more afraid of the ship than they are of the plantations."

The convicts were in the course of an hour or two ranged up against the bulwarks forward, and they were with much effort sufficiently browbeaten to bring them into some kind of order.

"They're a sorry lot of Newgate birds," said the captain to the mate. "I'm afraid we'll have a time of it before we change 'em off for merchantable tobacco. Here, you Cappy," he said to one of the older convicts. "Look here! Don't you tell anybody to-day that you're a

25

seaman. They'll swear you are a pirate, and that you'll be off with one of their country sloops, and go a-blackbearding it down the coast. You're to be a schoolmaster to-day."

"I can't read much, and I can't hardly write a word," said the man, a burly fellow of about sixty, whose heavy jaws and low brows would look brutal in spite of the brand-new periwig put on him that very morning to make him salable.

"That don't matter," said the captain. "You're schoolmaster enough for a tobacco country. You can navigate a ship by the sun and compass, and that's education enough. If you go and let it out that you're a sailor, I'll—well, you've been a captain or mate, and you know devilish well what I'll do with you. I'll serve you as you have served many a poor devil in your time."

Then, catching sound of a quarrel between two of the women, the captain called the mate, and said: "Give both of the wenches a touch off with your rope's end. Don't black their eyes or hit 'em about the face, but let 'em just taste the knot once over the shoulders to keep 'em peaceable. Be in haste, or they'll scratch one another's eyes."

The mate proceeded to salute the two women with a sharp blow apiece of the knotted rope, and thus changed their rising fury into sullenness.

Planters came and went during the forenoon, and cross-questioned the convicts, threatening to make it hard for them if they did not tell the truth. The visitors drank the captain's bumbo, but the convicts were slow of sale. Some of the planters announced their intention not to buy any more convicts, meaning for the future to purchase only freewillers, or bond servants voluntarily selling themselves, and some had made up their minds not to buy any more Christian servants at all, but to stock their places with blacks.

It was mid-afternoon when Sanford Browne arrived in his dugout, propelled against a head wind and heavy seas by Bob, the white redemptioner, and Jocko, the negro boy. The planter himself sat astern steering, with little Sanford crouched between his knees. Leaving the two servants in the canoe, the planter and his son went aboard the ship, while the convicts crowded against the guard rail to get a look at the naked figure of Jocko, his black skin being a novel sight to their English eyes.

There was recognition between the captain of the Nancy Jane, who had sailed to the Potomac for many years, and Sanford Browne. While the two stood in conversation by the bowl of strong rum punch, little Sanford strolled about the deck, shyly scrutinizing the faces of the convicts and being scrutinized by them. The women tried to talk with him, but their rather battered countenances frightened the boy, and he slipped away. At last he planted himself before old Cappy, whose bronzed face under a new powdered wig produced a curious effect.

"Where did you come from?" demanded the child, with awakened curiosity.

The would-be schoolmaster started at this question, gazed a moment at the child, and said, "God!" between his teeth.

"Lawr! 'e's one uv yer scholars, Cappy," said one of the women, in derision. "Ye'll be a-l'arnin' 'im lots uv words 'e ain't never 'eerd uv afore. Yer givin' the young un a prime lesson in swearin' to begin."

But Cappy made no reply. He only looked more eagerly at the child, and wiped his brow with his sleeve, disarranging his periwig in doing so. Then, changing the form of his exclamation but not its meaning, he muttered, "The devil!"

"W'atever's the matter?" said the woman. "You're fetching in God an' the devil both. Is the young un one uv yer long-lost brothers, Cappy?"

"What's your name?" demanded Cappy of the boy, without heeding the woman's gabble.

"Sanford Browne."

The perspiration stood in beads on the man's forehead, and the veins were visibly distended. "Looks like as if he hadn't got any bigger in more'n twenty years," he soliloquized. Then he said to the boy in an eager whisper, for his voice was dry and husky, "What's yer pappy's name, lad?"

"He's Sanford Browne, too. That's him a-talking to Captain Jackson at t'other end of the ship. He was stole when he was a little

27

boy by a mean old captain, and brought over here and sold, just like you folks," and the lad made the remark general by looking around him. "He's got rich now, and he's got more'n a thousand acres of land," said the little Sanford, boastfully, thinking perhaps that his father's success might encourage the woe-begone set before him. "But I reckon that mean old captain'll ketch it if pappy ever sets eyes on to him," he added.

"Lawr! now w'atever's the matter uv you, Cappy?" put in the woman again. "A body'd think you must 'a' been that very cap'n yer own self."

The man turned fiercely upon the garrulous woman and seized her throat with his left hand, while he threatened her with a clenched fist and growled like a wild beast. "Another word of that, Poll, and I'll knock the life out of you."

Poll gave a little shriek, which brought the mate on the scene with his threatening rope's end, and restored Cappy to a sort of self-control, though with a strange eagerness of terror his eyes followed the frightened lad as he retreated toward his father.

The planter, after discussing with Captain Jackson the death of the Prince of Wales in the preceding March, was explaining to the captain that he did not mean to buy any more white servants. The blacks were better, and were good property, while the black children added to a planter's estate. White servants gave you trouble, and in four or seven years at most their time expired, and you had to break in new ones. But still, if he could pick up a fellow that would know how to sail his sloop in a pinch, he might buy.

"There's one, now," said Captain Jackson; "that chap leaning on the capstan; he's been a captain, I believe."

"How'd they come to convict a captain?" demanded the planter, laughing. "We planters have always thought that all captains were allowed to steal a little."

"They mustn't steal from their owners," said Captain Jackson good-naturedly. "Passengers and shippers we do clip a little when we can, but that old fool must have tried to get something out of the owners of the ship. He's too old to run away now, or cut up any more deviltry. Go and talk with him."

"What's his bob-wig for?"

"Oh, that's some of my mate's nonsense. He thought planters wouldn't want to buy a seaman, so he rigged the old captain up like a schoolmaster, and told him to say that he had always taught arithmetic. He'll tell you he's a schoolmaster, according to the mate's commands; but he isn't. He's been a ship's captain, I believe, and he helped me take observations on the voyage, and he seemed to know the river when he got in last night."

There ensued some talk as to how many hogsheads of tobacco the convict was worth, and then Browne went forward to inspect the man and question him.

"What's your name?" said the planter.

"James Palmer," said Cappy, with his head down.

"Lawr!" muttered Polly under her breath.

"What's your business?"

"Schoolmaster."

"Come, don't lie to me," said Browne. "You are a sailor, or a captain maybe."

This set the old fellow to trembling visibly, and Polly again said "Lawr!" loud enough for him to hear it and give her one fierce glance that quieted her.

"Who said I was a sailor, sir?"

"Captain Jackson."

"That's because you want a sailor," stammered the convict. "Mighty little I ever knew about a ship till I got aboard this thing. Captain would 'a' told you I was a carpenter or a preacher if he thought that was what you wanted."

The man spoke gaspingly, and a dim sense of having known him began to make its way into the mind of the planter. He was going to ask him where he had taught school, but all at once a rush of memories crowded his mind, and a strange suspicion came to him. He stood silent and staring at the convict half a minute. Then he walked round him, examining him from this side and that.

"Let me see your left hand, you villain!" he muttered, approaching the man.

The convict had kept his left hand shoved down under his belt. He shook now as with an ague, and made no motion.

29

"Out with it!" cried the planter.

Slowly the old man drew out his hand, showing that one joint of the little finger was gone.

"You liar!" said the planter, at the same time pulling the bob-wig from the convict's head, and flinging it on the deck. "Your name is not James Palmer, but Jim Lewis, Captain Jim Lewis of the Red Rose—'Black Jim,' as everybody called you behind your back!"

Here Poll broke out again with "Lawr!" while Sanford Browne paused, fairly choked with emotion. Then he began again in a low voice:

"You thought I wouldn't know you. I've been watching out for you these ten years, to send you to hell with my own hands! You robbed my poor mother of her boy." The wretch cowered beneath the planter's gaze, and essayed to deny his identity, but his voice died in his throat. Browne at length turned on his heel, and strode rapidly toward the captain.

"I'll take him at the price you fixed," he called out as he advanced.

The captain wondered what gold mine Browne had discovered in Cappy to make him so eager to accept the first price named. He for his part was equally eager to be rid of a convict whom he regarded as rather a dangerous man, so he said promptly, "He belongs to you," and shook hands according to the custom in "closing a bargain."

A moment later Black Jim Lewis, having regained his wits, rushed up to the captain entreating hoarsely not to be sold to Browne. "Now, don't let him have me, Captain Jackson; for God's sake, don't, now! He's my enemy. He'll beat me and starve me to death. I'm one of your own kind; I'm a sea captain, and it's a shame for you, a sea captain too, to sell me to a man that hates me and only wants to make me miserable. I'm ruinated anyhow, and you ought to take some pity on me."

This plea for a freemasonry among sea captains had influence with the captain of the Nancy Jane. But he said, "W'y, Jim Lewis, I've sold to you the best master in the province of Maryland. You don't know when you're well off. Mr. Browne feeds his people well, and he never beats 'em bad, like the rest."

"I tell you, he'll flay me alive, that man will! You'd better shoot me dead and put me out of misery."

While the wretch was making this appeal, Browne was silently engaged in emptying the priming of his flintlock fowling piece, picking open the tube, and then filling the pan with fresh powder from the horn at his side. When he had closed the pan, he struck the stock of the gun one or two blows to shake the powder well down into place, that the gun might not miss fire. Then turning to the captain, he said, "A bargain is a bargain."

Then to the convict he said: "Black Jim Lewis, you belong to me. Get into that boat, or it'll be worse for you," and he slowly raised the snaphance with his thumb on the hammer.

Lewis had aged visibly in ten minutes. With trembling steps he walked to the ship's side, and clambered over the bulwarks into the dugout. The boy followed, and then the master took his seat in the stern, with his flintlock fowling piece within reach.

"My dead body'll float down here past the Nancy Jane," said Jim Lewis to the captain; "and I'll ha'nt your ship forever—see if I don't!" He half rose and waved his hand threateningly as he said this in a hoarse, sepulchral voice.

"Mr. Browne," interposed the captain of the Nancy Jane, as the lifted canoe paddles were ready to dip into the water, "don't be too hard on the old captain. You see how old and shaken he is. You'll show moderation, now, won't you?"

"I'll care for him," answered Browne unbendingly. "Away with the canoe! Good-by, captain. My tobacco will be ready for you."

And Poll, the convict, as she leaned over the rail and watched the fast-receding canoe pitching up and down on the seas, said, "Lawr!"

SCENE III

The time is the late afternoon of the same day, and the place is again Sanford Browne's plantation.

Judith Browne, having exhausted her experiments on the frock, the bonnet, and the hoop petticoat bought for her in London and sent like the proverbial pig in a poke, had taken to watching the Yankee peddling sloop, which, having lain for an hour at Patterson's on the Virginia shore, was now heading for the Browne place. It was pretty to see the sloop heel over under a beam wind and shoot steadily forward, while the waves dashed fair against her weather side and splashed the water from time to time to the top of her free board. It was a pleasant sight to mark her approach by the gradual increase in her size and the growing distinctness with which the details of her rigging could be made out. At length, when her bow appeared to Judith Browne to be driving so straight on the bank that nothing could prevent the vessel's going ashore Captain Perkins called to his only man, standing at the helm, "Hard down!" and the sloop swung her nose into the waves, and gracefully rounded head into the wind just in time to lie close under the bank, rocking fore and aft like a duck. As soon as she had swung into the wind enough for her sail to flap, the captain called to the boy who was the third member of the crew to let go the halyards; and as the sail ran rattling down, the captain heaved the anchor at the bow with his own hands. Then a plank was run out, a line made fast forward, and Perkins climbed the bank and greeted Mrs. Browne. His manner combined strangely the heartiness of the seaman with the sinuous deference of the peddler. His speech was that which one hears only in the most up-country New England regions and among London small shopkeepers. The uttering of his vowel sounds taper end first greatly amused his customers in the Chesapeake regions, while their abrupt clipping of both vowels and liquids was equally curious to Perkins, who regarded all people outside of New England as natives to be treated with condescending kindness alike for Christian and for business reasons, and as people who were even liable to surprise him by the possession of some rudimentary virtues in spite of their unlucky outlandishness.

"Glad to see yeh again, Mis' Braown," he said when he reached the top of the bank. "Where's Mr. Braown?"

"He's gone down to the Nancy Jane. Won't you come in, Captain Perkins? Come in and sit down a while."

"Wal, yes. And how's your little gal?" Seeing a dubious look on Mrs. Browne's face, he said: "Or is it a boy, now? I call at so many houses I git confused. Fine child, I remember."

"The lad's gone off with his father," said Judith, giving Perkins a seat in the passage.

After more preliminary talk the peddler got to his main point, that he had lots of nice notions and things this year cheaper'n they could be had in London. All the folks agreed that his things were "cheaper, considerin' quality, Mis' Braown, than you could git 'em in London."

Judith knew by experience that his things were neither very good nor very cheap, but her only chance in life to know anything of the delights of shopping lay in the coming of peddling sloops. One might order a frock, a bonnet, or a petticoat from London, but one must wait nearly a year till the tobacco ship returned to get what had been sent for. It was better to be cheated a little in order to get the pleasure of making up her mind and then changing it, of fancying herself possessor now of this and now of that, and finally getting what she liked best after having had the usufruct of the whole stock. She was soon examining the goods that Perkins's boy had brought up to her—fancy things for herself and young Sanford, and coarse cloth for her servants. She concluded nothing about staple trading till her husband should return; for prices were to be fixed on the corn and bacon which must be paid in exchange. But there were articles that she craved, and of which she preferred not to speak to her husband, for a while at least, and these she paid for from her little hoard of pieces of eight, or Spanish dollars. The change she made in fractions of these coins—actual quarters of dollars cut like pieces of pie. These were tested in Perkins's little money scales. Less than a quarter of a dollar was usually disregarded in the South; and as for Perkins, he never seemed to have any fractional silver to give back in change, but always proposed some little article that he would put in at cost just to fill up to the value of a piece of eight.

33

Paddling with the wind, Sanford Browne's cedar canoe made good speed, and as the sun was setting and the wind falling it glided past the Yankee sloop into shoal water farther up, where its inmates disembarked, and beached their craft.

Sanford Browne walked rapidly up the bank, followed by his son, the servants, and the old convict. He approached Perkins and greeted him, but in a manner not cordial and hardly courteous. He looked at Judith so severely that she fancied him offended with her. She reflected quickly that he could not have known anything of her surreptitious trading with the peddler. Uriah Perkins concluded that a storm was brewing between husband and wife, and found it necessary to return to the sloop to make her fast astern, against the turn of the tide and the veering of the wind.

When Perkins had disappeared, Sanford Browne pointed to the convict and said slowly and with fierceness:

"Judy, that's the man. That's Black Jim Lewis, that stole me away from home and sold me for a redemptioner. Jocko, go fetch the manacles."

Judith stood speechless. It was a guiding maxim with her that women should not meddle with men's business, and it was an article of faith that whatever her husband did was right. She sympathized with his resentment against the man who had kidnaped him. But the sight of the terror-stricken face of the cowardly brute smote her woman's heart with pity as the manacles were put on the convict's wrists.

"See that he doesn't get away," said Browne to Bob.

"He can't pound his corn with them things," said Bob, pointing to the handcuffs. "Shall I get him some meal?"

"Not to-night," said Browne. "He didn't give me a crust to eat the first night I was on ship. Turn about's fair play, Captain Lewis. Take him to the quarters."

When the convict found himself manacled, his terror increased. He pulled away from Bob and approached Browne.

"Let me speak a word, master," he began tremulously. "I'm all broke up and ruinated, anyhow. I know the devil must 'a' been in me the day I took you away. I've thought of it many a time, and I've said, 'Jim Lewis, something dreadful'll come to you for stealin' a good little boy that way.'" Here he paused. Then he resumed in a still more broken voice: "When I was put on to a transport to come to this country I remembered you, and I says, 'That's what's come of it.' Soon as I saw that little fellow, the very picture of you the day when I coaxed you away, I says to myself, 'O my God, I'm done fer now! I'm ruinated for a fact; I might as well be in hell as in Maryland.' But, master, if you'll only have just a little pity on an old man that's all broke up and ruinated, I'll—I'll—be a good servant to you. I promise you, afore Almighty God. Don't you go and be too hard on a poor ruinated old man. I'm old—seems to me I'm ten year older than I wuz afore I saw you this mornin'. I know you hate me. You've got strong reasons to hate me. I hate myself, and I keep sayin' to myself, says I, 'Jim Lewis, what an old devil you are!' But please, master, if you won't be too hard on me, I think I'll be better. I can't live long nohow. But——"

"There, that'll do," said Browne.

"Please, Mr. Browne," interposed Judy.

"Lewis, do you remember when you woolded a sailor's head?" demanded the planter.

"I don't know, master. I have done lots of things a little hard. Sailors are a hard lot."

"If you'd had pity on that poor sailor when he begged for mercy, I'd have pity on you to-night But I cried over that sailor that you wouldn't have mercy on, and now I can't pity you a bit. You've made your own bed. Your turn has come."

Saying this, Sanford Browne went into the house, while the old sea captain followed Bob in a half-palsied way round the south end of the house toward the servants' quarters, muttering, "Well, now, Jim Lewis, you're done fer."

"Mr. Browne, what are you going to do with that old man?" asked Judy, with more energy than she usually showed in speaking to her husband.

"I don't know, Judy. Something awful, I reckon." Browne could not make up his mind to any distinct act of cruelty beyond sending the convict supperless to bed.

"I don't like you to be so hard on an old man. I know he's bad—as bad as can be, but that's no reason why you should be bad."

"I wouldn't be bad, Judy. Just think how he sold me, like Joseph, away from my family!"

"But Joseph wasn't really very unkind to his brothers, Mr. Browne; and you won't be too hard on the poor old wretch, now will you?"

"Judy, I mean to make him suffer. When I think of my mother, and all she must have suffered, I haven't a drop of pity in me. He's got to suffer for his crimes now. That's what he was thrown into my hands for, I reckon, Judy."

"Then you won't be the man you have been. Time and again you've bought some poor kid from a hard master like old Hoak, to save him from suffering. Now you'll get to be hard and hateful like old Hoak yourself."

"Judy, remember my mother."

"Do you think your mother, if she is alive, would like to think of your standing over that old wretch while he was whipped and whipped and washed with salt water, maybe? If your mother has lived, she has been kept alive just by thinking what a good boy you were; and she says to herself, 'My Sanford wouldn't hurt anything. If he was run off to the plantations, he has grown to be the best man in all the country.' Do you think she'd like to have you turn a kind of public whipper or hangman for her sake?"

Browne looked at his wife in surprise. Her eyes flashed as she spoke, and the little womanly body, whose highest flight had seemed to end in a London frock and petticoat, had suddenly become something much more than he had fancied possible to her. She had taken the first place, and he felt himself overshadowed. He looked up at her with a sort of reverence, but he held stubbornly to a purpose that had been ossifying for twenty years.

"That's all well enough for a woman, Judy. But you know that any other man would do just what I am going to do, under the same circumstances. I don't like to do what you don't want me to do, but I sha'n't let old Lewis off. I reckon he'll find my hand hard

36

on him as long as he holds out. Any other man would do just the same, Judy."

Judith Browne stood still and looked at her husband in silence. Then she spoke in a repressed voice:

"Sanford Browne, what do you talk to me that way for? Any other man might worry this old wretch out of his life, but you won't do it. What did I marry you for? Why did I leave my father's house to take you, a poor redemptioner just out of your time? It was because you weren't like other men. I knew you were kind and good-hearted when other men were cruel and unfeeling. From that day to this you have never made me sorry that I left home and turned my father against me. But if you do this thing you have in mind to a poor old wretch that can't help himself, then you won't be Sanford Browne any more. You'll have that old man's blood on your hands, and Judy will never get over being sorry that she left her friends to go with you." The woman's voice had broken as she spoke these last words, and now she broke down completely, and sobbed a little.

"What shall I do, Judy?" said her husband softly. "God knows, if I keep him in sight I shall kill him some day."

"Sell him. Sell him right off. There's Captain Perkins coming up the bank now."

"You sell him, Judy. Perkins has things you want. I give Lewis to you. Make any trade you please." Then, as his wife moved away, he followed her, and said in a smothered voice: "Sell him quick, Judy. Don't stand on the price. Get him out of sight before I kill him."

Judith went out to meet the peddling captain, who was now strolling toward the house in hope of an invitation to supper, knowing that Mrs. Browne's biscuit and fried chicken were better than the salt pork and hoecake cooked by the boy on the sloop. The wind had fallen, and the water view was growing dim in the gloaming. Judith explained to the peddler that the convict her husband had bought proved to be an old enemy of his. She stammered a little in her endeavor not to betray the real reasons for selling him, and Perkins, who was proud of his own penetration, inferred that Browne was afraid of his life if he should keep the new servant. He saw in this an unexpected chance for profit. When Mrs. Browne offered to sell him if Perkins would take him to the eastern shore or some other place away off, he said that servants wuz a thing he didn't deal in—a leetle dangerous at sea where the crew wuz so small as his. Hard to sell an old fellow; the planters wanted young men. But he wanted to accommodate, you know, an' seein' as how Mis' Braown had been a good customer, he would do what he could. He would have to make a run over to the eastern shore perticular to sell this man. Folks on the eastern shore didn't buy much. Hadn't sold 'em a hat, for instance. They all wore white cotton caps, men an' women; an' they made the caps themselves out of cotton of their own raisin'. But, as he wuz a-sayin', Mis' Braown had been a good customer, an' he wanted to accommodate. But he'd have to put the price low enough so as he wouldn't be poorer by the trade. Thus he faced about on his disjunctive conjunction, now this way, now that, until he had time to consider what was the very lowest figure he could offer as a basis for his higgling. He couldn't offer much, but he would give a price which he named in pieces of eight, stipulating that he should pay it in goods. He saw in this a chance for elastic profits in both directions.

Judith hardly gave a thought to the price he named; but as soon as she perceived that he had disentangled himself from his higgling preamble so far as to offer a definite sum, she accepted it.

This lack of hesitation on her part disconcerted the peddler, who had a feeling that a bargain made without preliminary chaffering had not been properly solemnized. He was suspicious now that he was the victim of some design.

"That is to say, Mis' Braown, I only dew this to accommodate ole friends. It ain't preudent to make such a trade in the dark. I'll dew it if I find the man sound in wind and limb, and all satisfactory, when I come to look him over."

"Of course that's what I mean," said Judith. "Now come in and take supper with us, captain," she continued, her voice still in a quiver with recent emotions.

"Well, I don't keer if I dew, jest fer to bind the bargain, you knaow. I told the boy I'd be back, but I reckon they won't wait long. Ship folks don't wait much on nobody."

Judith turned toward the house, followed by the peddler. Sanford Browne was still sitting in the entry just as Judith had left him, surprised and in a sense paralyzed by the sudden and effective opposition which his wife had offered to the gratification of his only grudge.

"Mr. Browne!" called Judith, almost hysterically, her tense nerves suddenly shaken again. "What's that? Something's happened down at the quarters."

Looking through the wide passage into the dim twilight beyond, she could see running figures like shadows approaching the house. Sanford Browne rose at his wife's summons in time to meet the convict Lewis, still manacled, as he rushed into the passage at the back of the house and dashed out again at the front. Browne attempted to arrest his flight, crying out, as he made an effort to seize him, "Stop, you old villain, or I'll kill you!" But the momentum of the flying figure rendered Browne's grasp ineffectual, and in a moment he was out of doors, just as Bob and Jocko and the other servants entered the passage in a pell-mell pursuit.

As the running man emerged from the darkness of the passage, Perkins, thinking his profit in jeopardy, threw himself athwart his path, and cried: "Here! Where be you a-goin' so fast with them things on your wrist?"

"To hell and damnation!" yelled Lewis, striking the peddler fair in the breast with both manacled hands, and sending him rolling on the ground.

The convict did not pause a moment in his flight, but, with the whole pack in full cry after him, dashed onward to the bank and down it. Before any of his pursuers could lay hands on him he was aboard the sloop.

"Ketch him! Ketch him!" cried Captain Perkins, once more on his feet, and giving orders from the top of the bank.

The cabin boy had just emerged from the cabin to call the man to supper. He and the sailor tried hard to seize the fleeing man, but Captain Lewis swerved to one side and ran round the gunwale of the sloop with both men after him. When he reached the stern he leaped beyond their reach, and plunged head first into the water, sinking out of sight where the fast-ebbing tide was now gurgling round the rudder.

In vain the boy and the sailorman looked with all their might at the place where he had gone down; in vain they poked a long pole into the water after him; in vain did Bob and Jocko paddle in the canoe all over the place where Black Jim Lewis had sunk.

Perkins took the precaution, before descending the bank, to say: "You'll remember, Mis' Braown, that I only bought him on conditions, and stipple-lated I wuz to be satisfied when I come to look him over. 'Tain't no loss of mine." This caveat duly lodged, he descended to the deck of his sloop, where he found the cabin boy shaking as with an ague.

"What be you a-trimblin' abaout, naow? Got a fever 'n' agur a'ready? Y' ain't afeard of a dead man, be yeh, Elkanah?"

"I don't noways like the idear," said Elkanah, "of sleepin' aboard, an' him dead thar by his own will, a-layin' closte up to the sloop."

"He ain't nowher's nigh the sloop," responded Perkins. "This ebb-tide's got him in tow, an' he'll be down layin' ag'in' the Nancy Jane afore mornin'. That's the ship he'll ha'nt, bein' kind uv used to her."

Browne had remained standing at the top of the bank, without saying a single word. He turned at last, and started slowly toward the house. Judith, forgetting her invitation to the peddler, went after her husband and took his hand.

"I'm so glad he's dead," said she. "I know the cruel man deserved his fate. He'll be off your mind, now, dear; and nobody can say you did it."

40

A BASEMENT STORY

I

It was one of those obscure days found only on the banks of Newfoundland. There was no sun, and yet no visible cloud; there was nothing, indeed, to test the vision by; there was no apparent fog, but sight was soon lost in a hazy indefiniteness. Near objects stood out with a distinctness almost startling. The swells ran high without sufficient provocation from the present wind, and attention was absorbed by the tremendous pitching of the steamer's bow, the wide arc described by the mainmast against no background at all, and by the smoky and bellying mainsail, kept spread to hold the vessel to some sort of steadiness in the waves. There was no storm, nor any dread of a storm, and the few passengers who were not seasick in stateroom bunks below, or stretched in numb passivity on the sofas in the music saloon, were watching the rough sea with a cheerful excitement. In the total absence of sky and the entire abolition of horizon the eye rejoiced, like Noah's dove, to find some place of rest; and the mainsail, smoky like the air, but cutting the smoky air with a sharp plane, was such a resting place for the vision. This sail and the reeky smokestack beyond, and the great near billows that emerged from time to time out of the gray obscurity—these seemed to save the universe from chaos. On such a day the imagination is released from bounds, individuality is lost, and space becomes absolute—the soul touches the poles of the infinite and the unconditioned.

I do not pretend that such emotions filled the breasts of all the twenty passengers on deck that day. One man was a little seasick, and after every great rushing plunge of the steamer from a billow summit into a sea valley he vented his irritation by wishing that he had there some of the poets that—here he paused and gasped as the ship balanced itself on another crest preparatory to another shoot down the flank of a swell, while the screw, thrown clean out of the water, rattled wildly in the unresisting air and made the ship quiver

41

in every timber—some of those poets, he resumed with bitterer indignation, that sing about the loveliness of the briny deep and the deep blue—but here an errant swell hit the vessel a tremendous blow on the broadside, making her roll heavily to starboard, and bringing up through the skylights sounds of breaking goblets thrown from the sideboards in the saloon below, while the passenger who hated marine poetry was capsized from his steamer chair and landed sprawling on the deck. A small group of young people on the forward part of the upper deck were passing the day in watching the swells and forecasting the effect of each upon the steamer, rejoicing in the rush upward followed by the sudden falling downward, much as children enjoy the flying far aloft in a swing or on a teetering see-saw, to be frightened by the descent. Some of the young ladies had books open in their laps, but the pretense that they had come on deck to read was a self-deluding hypocrisy. They had left their elderly relatives safely ensconced in staterooms below, and had worked their way up to the deck with much care and climbing and with many lurches and much grievous staggering, not for the purpose of reading, but to enjoy the society of other young women, and of such young men as could sit on deck. When did a young lady ever read on an ocean steamer, the one place where the numerical odds are reversed and there are always found two gallant young men to attend each young girl? This merry half dozen, reclining in steamer chairs and muffled in shawls, breathed the salt air and enjoyed the chaos into which the world had fallen. On this deck, where usually there was a throng, they felt themselves in some sense survivors of a world that had dropped away from them, and they enjoyed their social solitude, spiced with apparent peril that was not peril.

The enthusiastic Miss Sylvia Thorne, who was one of this party, was very much interested in the billows, and in the attentions of a student who sat opposite her. From time to time she remarked also on some of the steerage passengers on the deck below; particularly was she interested in a young girl who sat watching the threatening swells emerge from the mist. Miss Sylvia spoke to the young lady alongside of her about that interesting young girl in the steerage, but her companion said she had so much trouble with the Irish at home that she could not bear an Irish girl even at sea. Her mother, she went on to say, had hired a girl who had proved most ungrateful, she had—but here a scream from all the party told that a sea of more than usual magnitude was running up against the port side. A minute later and all were trying to keep their seats while the ship reeled away to starboard with vast momentum, and settled swiftly again into the trough of the sea.

Miss Thorne now wondered that the sail, which did not flap as she had observed sails generally do, in poems, did not tear into shreds as she had always known sails to do in novels when there was a rough sea. But the blue-eyed student, having come from a fresh-water college, and being now on a homeward voyage, knew all about it, and tried to explain the difference between a sea like this and a storm or a squall. He would have become hopelessly confused in a few minutes more had not a lucky wave threatened to capsize his chair and so divert the conversation from the sail to himself. And just as Sylvia was about to change back to the sail again for the sake of relieving his embarrassment, her hat strings, not having been so well secured as the sail, gave way, and her hat went skimming down to the main deck below, lodged a minute, and then took another flight forward. It would soon have been riding the great waves on its own account, a mark for curious sea gulls and hungry sharks to inspect, had not the Irish girl that Sylvia had so much admired sprung to her feet and seized it as it swept past, making a handsome "catch on the fly." A sudden revulsion of the vessel caused her to stagger and almost to fall, but she held on to the hat as though life depended on it. The party on the upper deck cheered her, but their voices could hardly have reached her in the midst of the confused sounds of the sea and the wind.

The student, Mr. Walter Kirk, a large, bright, blond fellow, jumped to his feet and was about to throw himself over the rail. It was a chance to do something for Miss Thorne; he felt impelled to recover her seventy-five-cent hat with all the abandon of a lover flinging himself into the sea to rescue his lady-love. But a sudden sense of the ludicrousness of wasting so much eagerness on a hat

43

and a sudden lurch of the ship checked him. He made a gesture to the girl who held the hat, and then ran aft to descend for it. The Irish girl, with the curly hair blown back from her fair face, started to meet Mr. Kirk, but paused abruptly before a little inscription which said that steerage passengers were not allowed aft. Then turning suddenly, she mounted a coil of rope, and held the hat up to Miss Thorne.

"There's your hat, miss," she said.

"Thank you," said Sylvia.

"Sure you're welcome, miss," she said, not with a broad accent, but with a subdued trace of Irish in the inflection and idiom.

When the gallant Walter Kirk came round to where the girl, just dismounted from the cordage, stood, he was puzzled to see her without the hat.

"Where is it?" he asked.

"The young lady's got it her own self," she replied.

Kirk felt foolish. Had his chum come down over the rail for it? He would do something to distinguish himself. He fumbled in his pockets for a coin to give the girl, but found nothing smaller than a half sovereign, and with that he could ill afford to part. The girl had meanwhile turned away, and Kirk had nothing left but to go back to the upper deck.

The enthusiastic Sylvia spoke in praise of the Irish girl for her agility and politeness, but the young lady alongside, who did not like the Irish, told her that what the girl wanted was a shilling or two. Servants in Europe were always beggars, and the Irish people especially. But she wouldn't give the girl a quarter if it were her hat. What was the use of making people so mean-spirited?

"I'd like to give her something, if I thought it wouldn't hurt her feelings," said Sylvia, at which the other laughed immoderately.

"Hurt her feelings! Did you ever see an Irish girl whose feelings were hurt by a present of money? I never did, though I don't often try the experiment, that's so."

"I was going to offer her something myself, but she walked away while I was trying to find some change," said Kirk.

The matter of a gratuity to the girl weighed on Sylvia

Thorne's mind. She had a sense of a debt in owing her a gratuity, if one may so speak. The next day being calm and fine, and finding her company not very attractive, for young Kirk was engaged with some gentlemen in a stupid game of shuffleboard, she went forward to the part of the deck on which the steerage passengers were allowed to sun themselves, and found the Irish girl holding a baby. "You saved my hat yesterday," she said with embarrassment.

"Sure that's not much now, miss. I'd like to do somethin' for you every day if I could. It isn't every lady that's such a lady," said the girl, with genuine admiration of the delicate features and kindly manner of young Sylvia Thorne.

"Does that baby belong to some friend of yours?" asked the young lady.

"No, miss; I've not got any friends aboard. Its mother's seasick, and I'm givin' her a little rest an' holdin' the baby out here. The air of that steerage isn't fit for a baby, now, you may say."

Should she give her any money? What was it about the girl that made her afraid to offer a customary trifle?

"Where did you live in Ireland?" inquired Sylvia.

"At Drogheda, miss, till I went to work in the linen mills."

"Oh! you worked in the linen mills."

"Yes, miss. My father died, and my mother was poor, and girls must work for their living. But my father wanted me to get a good bit of readin' and writin' so as I might do better; but he died, miss, and I couldn't leave my mother without help."

"You were the only child?"

"I've got a sister, but somehow she didn't care to go out to work, and so I had to go out to service; and I heard that more was paid in Ameriky, where I've got an aunt, an' I had enough to take me out, an' I thought maybe I'd get my mother out there some day, or I'd get money enough to make her comfortable, anyways."

"What kind of work will you do in New York? I don't believe we've got any linen mills. I think we get Irish linen table-cloths, and so on."

"Oh, I'm going out to service. I can't do heavy work, but I can do chambermaid's work."

All this time Sylvia was turning a quarter over in her pocket. It was the only American coin she had carried with her through Europe, and she now took it out slowly, and said:

"You'll accept a little something for your kindness in saving my hat."

"I'm much obliged, miss, but I'd rather not I'd rather have your kind words than any money. It's very lonesome I've been since I left Drogheda."

She put the quarter back into her pocket with something like shame; then she fumbled her rings in a strange embarrassment. She had made a mess of it, she thought. At the same time she was glad the girl had so much pride.

"What is your name?" she asked.

"Margaret Byrne."

"You must let me help you in some way," said Miss Thorne at last.

"I wonder what kind of people they are in New York, now," said Margaret, looking at Sylvia wistfully. "It seems dreadful to go so far away and not know in whose house you'll be livin'."

Sylvia looked steadily at the girl, and then went away, promising to see her again. She smiled at Walter Kirk, who had finished his game of shuffleboard and was looking all up and down the deck for Miss Thorne. She did not stop to talk with him, however, but pushed on to where her mother and father were sitting not far from the taffrail.

"Mamma, I've been out in the steerage."

"You'll be in the maintop next, I don't doubt," said her father, laughing.

"I've been talking to the Irish girl that caught my hat yesterday."

"You shouldn't talk to steerage people," said Mrs. Thorne. "They might have the smallpox, or they might not be proper people."

"I suppose cabin passengers might have the smallpox too," said Mr. Thorne, who liked to tease either wife or daughter.

"I offered the Irish girl a quarter, and she wouldn't have it."

46

"You're too free with your money," said her mother in a tone of complaint that was habitual.

"The girl wouldn't impose on you, Sylvia," said Mr. Thorne. "She's honest. She knew that your hat wasn't worth so much. Now, if you had said fifteen cents— —"

"O papa, be still," and she put her hand over his mouth. "I want to propose something."

"Going to adopt the Irish— —" But here Sylvia's hand again arrested Mr. Thorne's speech.

"No, I'm not going to adopt her, but I want mamma to take her for upstairs girl when we get home."

Mr. Thorne made another effort to push away Sylvia's hand so as to say something, but the romping girl smothered his speech into a gurgle.

"I couldn't think of it. She's got no references and no character."

"Maybe she has got her character in her pocket, you don't know," broke out the father. "That's where some girls carry their character till it's worn out."

"I'll give her a character," said Sylvia. "She is a lady, if she is a servant."

"That's just what I don't want, Sylvia," said Mrs. Thorne, with a plaintive inflection, "a ladylike servant."

"Oh, well, we must try her. How's the girl to get a character if nobody tries her? And she's real splendid, I think, going off to get money to help her mother. And I'm sure she's had some great sorrow or disappointment, you know. She's got such a wistful look in her face, and when I spoke about Drogheda she said— —"

"There you are again!" exclaimed the father. "You'll have a heroine to make your bed every morning. But you'd better keep your drawers locked for all that."

"Now, I think that's mean!" and the young girl tried to look stern. But the severity vanished when Mr. Kirk, of the senior class in Highland College, came up to inform Miss Thorne that the young people were about getting up a conundrum party. Miss Sylvia accepted the invitation to join in that diluted recreation, saying, as she departed, "Let's try her anyway."

47

"If she wants her I suppose I shall have to take her, but I wish she had more sense than to go to the steerage for a servant."

"She could hardly find one in the cabin," ventured Mr. Thorne.

So it happened that, on arrival in New York, Margaret Byrne was installed as second girl at the Thornes'. For in an American home the authority is often equitably divided—the mother has the name of ruling the household which the daughter actually governs.

II

How much has the setting to do with a romance? The old tales had castles environed with savage forests and supplied with caves and underground galleries leading to where it was necessary to go in the novelist's emergency. In our realistic times we like to lay our scenes on a ground of Axminster with environments of lace curtains, pianos, and oil paintings. How, then, shall I make you understand the real human loves and sorrows that often have play in a girl's heart, where there are no better stage fittings than stationary washtubs and kitchen ranges?

Sylvia Thorne was sure that the pretty maid from Drogheda, whose melancholy showed itself through the veil of her perfect health, had suffered a disappointment. She watched her as she went silently about her work of sweeping and bedmaking, and she knew by a sort of divination that here was a real heroine, a sufferer or a doer of something.

Mrs. Thorne pronounced the new maid good, but "awfully solemn." But when Maggie Byrne met the eyes of Sylvia looking curiously and kindly at her sad face, there broke through her seriousness a smile so bright and sunny that Sylvia was sure she had been mistaken, and that there had been no disappointment in the girl's life.

Maggie shocked Mrs. Thorne by buying a shrine from an image vender and hanging it against the wall in the kitchen. The mistress of the house, being very scrupulous of other people's

48

superstitions, and being one of the stanchest of Protestants, doubted whether she ought to allow an idolatrous image to remain on the wall. She had read the Old Testament a good deal, and she meditated whether she ought not, like Jehu, the son of Nimshi, to break the image in pieces. But Mr. Thorne, when the matter was referred to him, said that a faithful Catholic ought to do better than an unfaithful one, and that so long as Margaret did not steal the jewelry she oughtn't to be disturbed at her prayers, which it was known she was accustomed to say every night, with her head bowed on the ironing table, before the image of Mary and her son.

"How can the Catholics pray to images and say the second commandment, I'd like to know?" said Mrs. Thorne, one morning, with some asperity.

"By a process like that by which we Protestants read the Sermon on the Mount, and then go on reviling our enemies and laying up treasures on earth," said her husband.

"My dear, you never will listen to reason; you know that the Sermon on the Mount is not to be taken literally."

"And how about the second commandment?"

"You'd defend the scribes and Pharisees, I do believe, just for the sake of an argument."

"Oh, no! there are plenty of them alive yet; let them defend themselves, if they want to," said the ungallant husband, with a wicked twinkle in his eye.

As for Sylvia, she was all the more convinced, as time went on, that the girl "had had a disappointment." On the evenings when the cook was out Sylvia would find her way into the kitchen for a talk with Maggie. The quaint old stories of Ireland and the enthusiastic description of Irish scenes that found their way into Margaret Byrne's talk delighted Sylvia's fancy. But the conversations always ended by some allusion to the ship and the hat, and to the large-shouldered blond young man that came down after the hat; and Sylvia confided to Maggie that he had asked permission to call to see her the next summer, when he should come East after his graduation. Margaret had no other company, and she regularly looked for Sylvia on the evenings when she was alone, brightening the kitchen for the occasion so much as to convince the "down-stairs girl" that sly Maggie was accustomed to receive a beau in her absence.

One evening Miss Thorne found Maggie in tears.

"I've a mind to tell you all about it," said the girl, in answer to the inquiries of Sylvia, at the same time pushing her hair back off her face and leaning her head on her hands while she rested her elbows on the table.

"Maybe it will do you good to tell me," answered Sylvia, concealing her eager curiosity behind her desire to serve Margaret.

"Well, you see, miss, my sister Dora is purty."

"So are you, Maggie."

"No, but Dora is a young thing, and kind of helpless, like a baby. I was the oldest, and that Dora was my baby, like. Well, Andy Doyle and me were always friends. I wish I hadn't never seen him. But he seemed to be the nicest fellow in the world. There was never anything said between him an' me, only—well—but I can't tell ye— you're so young—you don't know about such things."

"Yes, I do. You loved him, didn't you?"

"You see, miss, he was always so good. Dora, she hadn't no end of b'ys that liked her. But anything that I had she always wanted, you may say, and I always 'umored her in a way. She was young and a kind of a baby, an' she is that purty, Miss Sylvy. Well, one of us had to go out to work in the mill, an' my mother, she said that Dora must go, because Dora wasn't any good about the house to speak of. She never knew how to do anything right. But Dora cried, and said she couldn't work in the mill, and so I went down to Larne to work in the mill, and Dora promised to look after the house. Now, at the time I went away Dora was all took up with Billy Caughey, and we thought sure as could be it was a match. But what does that girl do but desave Billy, and catch Andy. I don't think, miss, that he ever half loved her, but then I don't know what she made him believe; and then, ye know, nobody ever could refuse Dora anything, with her little beggin', winnin' ways. She just dazed him and got him engaged to her; and I don't believe he was ever entirely happy with her. But what could I do, miss? I couldn't try to coax him back—now could I? She was such a baby of a thing that she would cry if Andy only talked to me a minute after I come home. And I didn't want to take him away from her. That was when the mill at Larne had shut up. And so I hadn't no heart to do anything more there; it seemed like I was dead; and I knowed that if I stayed there would be trouble, for I could see that Andy looked at me strange, like there was somethin' he didn't quite understand, ye may say; but I was mad, and I didn't want to take away Dora's beau, nor to have anything to do with a lad that could change his mind so easy. And so I come away, thinkin' maybe I'd get some heart again on this side of the sea, and that I could soon send for me old mother to come."

Here she leaned her head on the table and cried.

"Now, there," she said after a while, "to-day I got a letter from Dora; there it is!" and she pushed it to the middle of the table as though it stung her. "She says that Andy is comin' over here to make money enough to bring her over after a while, sure. It kind o' makes my heart jump up, miss, to think of seein' anybody from Drogheda, and more'n all to see Andy again, that always played with me, and—— But I despise him too, miss, fer bein' so changeable. But then, Dora she makes fools out of all of them with her purty face and her coaxin' ways, miss. She can't help it, maybe."

"Well, you needn't see Andy if you don't want to," said Sylvia.

"Oh! but I do want to," and Margaret laughed through her tears at her own inconsistency. "Besides, Dora wants me to help him get a place, and I must do that; and then, sure, miss, do you think I'd let him know that I cared a farthin' fer him? Not a bit of it!" and Maggie pushed back her hair and held herself up proudly.

The next morning, as Margaret laid the morning paper on Mr. Thorne's table in the library, she ventured to ask if he knew of a place for a friend of hers that was coming from Ireland the next week. That gentleman had caught the infection of Sylvia's enthusiasm for the Irish girl, and by the blush on her cheek when she made the request he was sure that his penetration had divined the girl's secret. So he made some inquiries about Andy, and, finding that he was "handy with tools," the merchant thought he could give him a place in his packing department.

51

It happened, therefore, that Sylvia rarely spent any more evenings in the kitchen. Instead of that, her little sister used to frequent it, for Andy was very ingenious in making chairs, tables, and other furniture for doll houses, and little Sophy thought him the nicest man in the world. Maggie was very cool and repellent to him, with little spells of relenting. Sometimes Andy felt himself so much snubbed that he would leave after a five minutes' call, in which event Maggie Byrne was sure to relax a little at the door, and Sylvia or Sophy was almost certain to find her in tears afterward.

Andy could not, perhaps, have defined his feelings toward Margaret. He could not resist the attraction of the kitchen, for was not Maggie his old playmate and the sister of Dora? Sure, there was no harm at all in a fellow's goin' to see, just once a week, the sister of his swateheart, when the ocean kept him from seein' his swateheart herself. But if Andy had been a man accustomed to analyze his feelings he might have inquired how it came that he liked his swateheart's sister better even than his swateheart herself.

One evening he had a letter from Dora, and he thought to cheer Margaret with good news from home. But she would not be cheered.

"Now what's the matter, Mag?" Andy said coaxingly. "Don't that fellow in Larne write to ye?"

"What fellow in Larne?" demanded Margaret with asperity.

"Why, him that used to be so swate when ye was a-workin' in the mill."

"Who told you that?"

"Oh, now, you needn't try to kape it from me! Don't you think I knew all about it? Do you think Dora wouldn't tell me, honey? Don't I know you was engaged to him before you left the mill at Larne? Has he gone an' desaved you now, Maggie? If he has, I don't wonder you're cross."

"Andy, that isn't true. I never had any b'y at Larne, at all."

"Now, what's the use denying it? That's always the way with you girls about such things."

"Andy Doyle, do you go out of this kitchen, and don't you never come back. I never desaved you in my life, and I won't have nobody say that I did."

52

A conflict of feeling had made Margaret irritable, and Andy was the most convenient object of wrath in the absence of Dora. Andy started slowly out through the hall; there he turned about, and said:

"Hold a bit, my poor Mag. Let me git me thoughts together. It's me's been desaved. If it hadn't 'a' been fer that fellow down at Larne there wouldn't never 'a' been anything betwixt me and Dora. And now — —"

"Don't you say no more, Andy. Dora's a child, and she wanted you. Don't ye give her up. If you give her up, and she, poor child, on the other sides of the water, I'll never respict ye — d'ye hear that, now, Andy? Only the last letter she wrote she said she'd break her heart if I let you fall in love with anybody else. The men's all fools now, anyhow, Andy, and some of them is bad, but don't you go and desave that child, that's a-breakin' her heart afther you. And don't ye believe as I ever keered a straw for ye, for I don't keer fer you, nor no other man a-livin'."

Andy stood still for some moments, trying in a dumb way to think what to do or say; then he helplessly opened the door and went out.

III

The next Thursday evening Andy did not come, and Margaret felt sorry, she could not tell why. But Sylvia came down into the lower hall, peered through the glass of the kitchen door, and, finding the maid sitting alone by the range, entered as of old. And to her Maggie Byrne, sore pressed for sympathy, told of her last talk with the comely young man.

"You see, miss, it would be too mean for me to take Dora's b'y away from her, fer he's the finest-lookin' and altogether the nicest young man anywhere about Drogheda; and Dora, she's always used to havin' the best of everything, and she always took anything that was mine, thinkin' she'd a right to it, and, bein' a weak and purty young thing, I s'pose she had, now, miss."

"I think she's mean, Maggie, and you're foolish if you don't take your own lover back again."

"And she on the other sides of the say, miss? And my own little sister that I packed around in me arms? She's full of tricks, but then she's purty, and she's always been used to havin' my things. At any rate, 'tain't meself as'll be takin' away what's hers, and she's trusted him to me, and she's away on the other sides of the water. At least not if I can help it, miss. And I pray fer help all the time. Besides, do you think I'd have Andy Doyle afther what's happened, even if Dora was out of the way?"

"I know you would," said Sylvia.

"I believe I would, miss, I'm such a fool. But then sometimes I despise him. If it wasn't fer me dear old mother, that maybe I'll never see again," and Maggie wiped her eyes with her apron, "I'd join the Sisters. I think maybe I have got a vocation, as they call it."

It was the very next evening after this interview that Bridget Monahan, the downstairs girl, gave Margaret a little advice.

"He's a foine young feller, now, Mag, but don't you be in no hurry to git married. You're afther havin' a nice face—a kind o' saint's face, on'y it's a thrifle too solemn to win the men. But if Andy should lave, ye might be afther doin' better, and ye might be afther doin' worruss now, Mag. But don't ye git married till ye've got enough to buy a brocade shawl. Ef ye don't git a brocade shawl afore you're married, niver a bit of a one'll ye be afther gittin' afthewards. Girls like us don't git no money afther they are married, and it's best to lay by enough to git a shawl beforehand now, Mag. That's me own plan."

A few weeks later Maggie was thrown into grief by hearing of the death of her mother. Of course she received sympathy from Sylvia. Andy, also having received a letter from Dora, ventured to call on Maggie to express in his sincerely simple way his sympathy for her grief, and to discuss with her what was now to be done for the homeless girl in the old country.

"We must bring her over, Andy."

"I know that," said the young man. "I'll draw all my money out of the Shamrock Savings Bank to-morry and send her a ticket.

But I'll tell you what, Mag, after I went away from here the last time I felt sure I'd never marry Dora Byrne. But maybe I was wrong. Poor thing! I'm sorry fer her, all alone."

"Sure, now, Andy, you must 'a' made a mistake," said Maggie. "It's myself as may've given Dora rason to think I'd got a young man down at Larne. I don't know as she meant to desave you. She needn't, fer you know I don't keer fer men, neither you nor anybody. I'm goin' into the Sisters, now my mother's dead. I've spoken to Sister Agnes about it."

But whether it was from her lonely feeling at the death of her mother, or from her exultation at her victory over her feelings, or whether it was that her heart, trodden down by her conscience, sought revenge, she showed more affection for Andy this evening than ever before, following him to the area gate, detaining him in conversation, and bidding him goodnight with real emotion.

The next evening Andy came again with a long face. He had a paper in which he showed Maggie an account of the suspension of the Shamrock Savings Bank, in which the money of so many Irishmen was locked up, and in which were all of Andy Doyle's savings, except ten dollars he had in his pocket.

"Now, Mag, what am I goin' to do? It takes thirty-five dollars for a ticket. If I put my week's wages that I'll git to-morry on to this, I'm short half of it."

"Sure, Andy, I'll let you have it all if you want it. You keep what you've got. She's me own sister. On'y I'll have to wait a while, for I don't want to fetch into the Sisters any less money than I've spoke to Sister Agnes about."

"I'm a-goin' to pay ye back every cint of it, Mag, and God bless ye! But it 'most makes me hate Dora to see you so good. And I tell you, Maggie, the first thing when she gits here she's got to explain about that fellow down at Larne that she told me about."

"Andy," said Maggie, "d'ye mind now what I say. I've suffered enough on account of Dora's takin' you away from me, but I'd rather die with a broken heart than to have anything to do with you if you are afther breakin' that poor child's heart when she comes here."

"Oh, then you did keer for me a little, Maggie darlint?" exclaimed Andy. "I thought you said you never did keer!"

Maggie was surprised. "I don't keer for you, nor any other man, and I never— —" But here she paused. "You ought to be ashamed to be talkin' that way to me, and you engaged to Dora. There, now, take the money, Andy, and git Dora's ticket, and don't let's hear no more foolish talkin' that it would break the poor dear orphan's heart to hear. The poor baby's got nobody but you and me to look afther her, now her mother's gone, and it's a shame and a sin if we don't do it."

IV

Margaret Byrne hurried her work through. The steamer that brought Dora had come in that day. Dora was met at Castle Garden by her aunt, and Margaret had got permission to go to see her in the evening. As Andy Doyle had to go the same way, he stopped for Maggie. All the way over to the aunt's house in Brooklyn he was moody and silent, the very opposite of a man going to meet his betrothed. Margaret was quiet, with the peace of one who has gained a victory. Her struggle was over. There was no more any danger that she should be betrayed into bearing off the affections of her sister's affianced lover.

Maggie greeted Dora affectionately, but Dora was like one distraught. She held herself aloof from her sister, and still more from Andy, who, on his part, made a very poor show of affection.

"Well," said Dora after a while, "I s'pose you two people have been afther makin' love to one another for six months."

"You hain't got any right to say that, Dora," broke out Andy. "Maggie's stood up fer you in a way you didn't more'n half desarve, and it's partly Maggie's money that brought you here. You know well enough what a—a—lie, if I must say it, you told me about Mag's havin' a beau at Larne, and she says she didn't. You're the one that took away your sister's— —" But here he paused.

"Hush up, Andy!" broke in Margaret. "You know I never

56

keered fer you, or any other man. Don't you and Dora begin to quarrel now."

Andy looked sullen, and Dora scared. At length Dora took speech timidly.

"Billy will be here in a minute."

"Billy who?" asked Andy.

"Billy Caughey," she answered. "He came over in the same ship with me."

"Oh, I s'pose you've been sparkin' with him ag'in! You pitched him over to take me— —"

"No, I haven't been sparkin' with him, Andy; at least, not lately. He's my husband. We got married three months ago."

"And didn't tell me?" said Andy, between pleasure and anger.

"No, we wanted to come over here, and we couldn't have come if it hadn't been for the money you sent."

"Why, Dora, how mean you treated Andy!" broke out Margaret.

"I knew you'd take up for him," said Dora pitifully, "but what could I do, sure? You won't hurt Billy, now, will you, Andy? He's afeard of you."

"Well," said Andy, straightening up his fine form with a smile of relief, "tell Billy that I wish him much j'y, and that I'll be afther thankin' him with all my heart the very first time I see him for the kindness he's afther doin' me. Good-night, Mrs. Billy Caughey, good luck to ye! As Mag says she don't keer fer me, I'll be after going home alone." This last was said bitterly as he opened the door.

"O Andy! wait fer me—do!" said Margaret.

"Ain't you stayin' to see Billy?" asked Dora.

"Not me. It's with Andy Doyle I'm afther goin'," cried Margaret, with a lightness she had not known for a year.

And the two went out together.

The next evening Margaret told Sylvia about it, and the little romance-maker was in ecstasy.

"So you won't enter the sisterhood, then?" she said, when Margaret had finished.

"No, miss, I don't think I've got any vocation."

THE GUNPOWDER PLOT

THE STORY OF A FOURTH OF JULY

Whenever one writes with photographic exactness of frontier life he is accused of inventing improbable things.

"Old Davy Lindsley" lived in a queer cabin on the Pomme de Terre River. If you should ever ride over the new Northern Pacific when it shall be completed, or over that branch of it which crosses the Pomme de Terre, you can get out at a station which will, no doubt, be called for an old settler, Gager's Station; and if you would like to see some beautiful scenery, take a canoe and float down the Pomme de Terre River. You will have to make some portages, and you will have a good appetite for supper when you reach the old Lindsley house, ten miles from Gager's, but its present owner is hospitable.

A queer old chap was Lindsley the last time I saw him. I remember how he took me all over his claim and showed me the beauties of Lindsleyville, as he called it. His long iron-gray hair fluttered in the wind, and his face seemed like a wizard's, penetrating but unearthly. That was long before the great tide of immigrants had begun to find their way into this paradise through the highway of the Sauk Valley. Lindsleyville was a hundred and fifty miles out of the world at that time. Its population numbered two—Lindsley and his daughter. The old man had tried to make a fortune in many ways. There was no sort of useless invention that he had not attempted, and you will find in the Patent Office models without number of beehives and cannons, steam cut-offs and baby jumpers, lightning churns and flying machines on which he had taken out patents, assured of making a fortune from each one. He had raised fancy chickens, figured himself rich on two swarms of bees, traveled with a magic lantern, written a philosophic novel, and started a newspaper. There was but one purpose in which he was fixed—which was, to guard his daughter jealously. To do this, and to make the experiment of building a Utopian city, he had

58

traveled to the summit of this knoll on the right bank of the Pomme de Terre. There never was a more beautiful landscape than that which Lindsleyville commanded. But the town did not grow, chiefly because it was so far beyond the border, though the conditions in his deeds intended to secure the character of the city from deterioration were so many that nobody would have been willing to buy the lots.

At the time I speak of David Lindsley had dwelt on the Pomme de Terre for five years. He had removed suddenly from the Connecticut village in which he had been living because he discovered that his daughter had, in spite of his watchfulness, formed an attachment for a young man who had the effrontery to disclose the whole thing to him by politely asking his consent to their marriage.

"Marry my daughter!" choked the old man. "Why, Mr. Brown, you are crazy! I have educated her upon the combined principles of Rousseau, of Pestalozzi, of Froebel, and of Herbert Spencer. And you—you only graduated at Yale, an old fogy mediæval institution! No, sir! not till I meet a philosopher whose mind has been symmetrically developed can I consent for my Emilia to marry."

And the old man became so frantic, that, to save him from the madhouse, Emilia wrote a letter, at his dictation, to young Brown, peremptorily breaking off all relations; and he, a sensitive, romantic man, was heartbroken, and left the village. He only sent a farewell to his friends the day before he was to sail from New Bedford on a whaling voyage. He carried with him the impression that an unaccountable change of mind in Emilia had left no hope for him.

To prevent a recurrence of such an untoward accident as this, and, as he expressed it, "to bring his daughter's mind into intimate relations with nature," the fanatical philosopher established the town of Lindsleyville, determined that no family in which there was a young man should settle on his town plot, unless, indeed, the young man should prove to be the paragon he was looking for.

Emilia's motherless life had not been a cheerful one, subjected to the ever-changing whims of a visionary father, with whom one of her practical cast of mind could have no point of sympathy. And since she came to Lindsleyville it was harder than ever, for there was no neighbor nearer than Gager's, ten miles away, and there was not a woman within fifty miles. There is no place so lonesome as a prairie; the horizon is so wide, and the earth is so empty!

Lindsley had spent all his own money long ago, and it was only the small annuity of his daughter, inherited from her mother's family, the capital of which was tied up to keep it out of his reach, that prevented them from starving. Emilia was starving indeed, not in body, but in soul. Cut off from human sympathy, she used to sit at the gable window of the cabin and look out over the boundless meadow until it seemed to her that she would lose her reason. The wild geese screaming to one another overhead, the bald eagles building in the solitary elm that grew by the river, the flocks of great white pelicans that were fishing on the beach of Swan Lake, three miles away, were all objects of envy to the lonesome heart of the girl; for they had companions of their kind—they were husbands and wives, and parents and children, while she—here she checked her thoughts, lest she should be disloyal to her father. To her disordered fancy the universe seemed to be a wheel. The sun and the stars came up and went down over the monotonous sea of grass with frightful regularity, and she could not tell whether there was a God or not. When she thought of God at all, it was as a relentless giant turning the crank that kept the sky going round. The universe was an awful machine. The prayers her mother taught her in infancy died upon her lips, and instead of praying to God she cried out to her mother. Un-protestant as the sentiment is, I can not forbear saying that this talking to the dead is one of the most natural things in the world. To Emilia the dimly remembered love of her mother was all of tenderness there was in the universe, the only revelation of God that had come to her, except the other love, which was to her a paradise lost. For the great hard fate that turned the prairie universe round with a crank motion had also—so it seemed to her—snatched away from her the object of her love. This disordered, faithless state was all the fruit she tasted of the peculiar education so much vaunted by her father. She had eaten the husks he gave her and was hungry.

60

I said she had no company. An old daguerreotype of her mother and a carefully hidden photograph (marked on the back, in a rather immature hand, "E. Brown") seemed to answer with looks of love and sympathy when she wetted them with her tears. They were her rosary and her crucifix; they were the gifts of a beclouded life, through which God shone in dimly upon her.

This poor girl looked and longed so for the company of human kind that she counted those red-letter days on which a half-breed voyageur traveled over the trail in front of the house, and even a party of begging and beggarly Sioux, hungry for all they could get to eat, offering importunately to sell "hompoes" (moccasins) to her father, were not wholly unwelcome. But the days of all days were those on which Edwards, the tall, long-haired American trapper, fished in the Pomme de Terre in sight of the Lindsley cabin. On such occasions the old man Lindsley would leave his work and stay about the house, and watch jealously and uneasily every movement of the trapper. On one or two occasions when that picturesque individual, wearing a wolf-skin cap, with the wolf's tail hanging down between his shoulders, presented himself at the door of the cabin to crave some little courtesy, Lindsley closed the front door and brought out the article asked for from the back, like a mediæval chieftain guarding his castle. But all the time that poor Emilia could hear the voice of the tall trapper her heart beat two beats for one. For was it not a human voice speaking her own language? And the days on which he was visible were accounted as the gates of paradise, and the moments in which he spoke in her hearing were as paradise itself.

This churlish, inhospitable manner made Lindsley many enemies in a land in which one can not afford to have enemies. Every half-breed hunter took the old man's suspicious manner as a personal affront. "He thinks we are horse thieves," they said scornfully. And Jacques Bourdon, the half-breed who had "filed on" the claim alongside Lindsley's, and even claimed unjustly a "forty" of Lindsley's town plot, had no difficulty in securing the sympathy of the settlers and nomads, who looked on Lindsley as a monster quite capable of anything. He was even reported to have beaten his daughter, and to have confined her in the wilderness that he might keep her out of an immense fortune which she had inherited. So Lindsley grew every day in disfavor in a region where unpopularity in its mildest form is sure to take a most unpleasant way of making itself known. Emilia knew enough to understand this danger, and she was shaken with a nameless fear whenever she heard the sharp words that passed between her father and Bourdon, the half-breed. The resentment of the latter reached its climax when the decision of the land office was rendered in favor of Mr. Lindsley. From that hour the revenge of this man, whose hot French was mixed with relentless Indian blood, hung over the head of the old man, who still read and wrote, and invented and theorized, in utter ignorance of any peril except the danger that some man, not a fool, should marry his daughter.

The Fourth of July was celebrated at Gager's. People came from fifty miles round. Patriotism? No! but love of human fellowship. The celebrated Pierre Bottineau and the other Canadians and half-breeds were there, mellowed with drink, singing the sensual and almost lewd French rowing songs their fathers had sung on the St. Lawrence. "Whisky Jim," the retired stage driver, and Hans Brinkerhoff and the other German settlers, with two or three Yankees, completed the slender crowd, which comprised almost the entire population of six skeleton counties. And the ever-popular Edwards was among them, his grave face and flowing ringlets rising above them all. A man so ready to serve anybody as he was idolized among frontiermen, whose gratitude is almost equal to their revenge. Captain Oscar, the popular politician, who wore his hair long and swore and drank, just to keep in with his widely scattered constituents, whom he represented in the Minnesota Senate each winter (and who usually cast half a dozen votes each for him), made a buncombe speech, and then Edwards, who wouldn't drink, but who knew how to tell strange stories, kept them laughing for half an hour. Edwards was a type of man not so uncommon on the frontier as those imagine who think the trapper always a half-horse, half-alligator creature, such as they read of in the Beadle novels. I knew one trapper who was a student of

62

numismatics, another who devoted his spare time to astronomy, and several traders and trappers who were men of considerable culture, though they are generally men who are a little morbid or eccentric in their mental structure. All Edwards's natural abilities, which were sufficient to have earned him distinction had he been "in civilization," were concentrated on the pursuits of his wild life, and such a man always surpasses the coarser and duller Indian or half-breed in his own field.

After a game of ball, and other sports imitated from the Indians, the bois brûlés[1] began to be too much softened with whisky to keep up athletic exercises, and something in their manner led Edwards to suspect that there were other amusements on the programme into the secret of which he had not been admitted.

By adroit management he contrived to overhear part of a conversation in which "poudre à canon" was mixed up with the name of Lindslee. He inferred that the blowing up of Lindsley's house was to finish the celebration of the national holiday. Treating Bourdon to an extra glass of whisky, and seasoning it with some well-timed denunciations of "the old monster," he gathered that the plan was to plant a keg of powder under the chimney on the north side of the cabin and blow it to pieces, just to scare the monster out, or kill him and his daughter, it did not matter which. Edwards praised the plan. He said that if it were not that he had to go to Pelican Lake that very night he would go along and help blow up the old rascal.

Soon after this he shook hands all around and wished them bon voyage in their trip to Lindsleyville. He winked his eyes knowingly, playing the hypocrite handsomely. Oscar and Bottineau left in different directions, the Germans had gone home drunk, and only "Whisky Jim" joined the half-breeds in their trip. They took possession of an immigrant team that was in Gager's stable, and just after sunset started on their patriotic errand. They were going to celebrate the Fourth by blowing up the tyrant.

Meantime Edwards had taken long strides, but his moccasin-

---

[1] Bois brûlés, "burnt wood," is the title the half-breeds apply to themselves, in allusion to their complexion.

clad feet were not carrying him in the direction of Pelican Lake. Half the time walking as only "the long trapper" could walk, half the time in a swinging trot, he made the best possible speed toward Lindsleyville. He had the start of the half-breeds, but how much he could not tell; and there was no time to be lost. At the summit of every knoll he looked back to see if they were coming, crouching in the grass lest they should discover him.

Lindsley received him as suspiciously as ever, and positively refused to believe his story. But by using his telescope Edwards soon convinced him that the party were just leaving Gager's. The dusk of the evening was coming on, and Lindsley's fright was great as he realized his daughter's peril.

"I will fight them to the death," he said, getting down his revolver, with an air that would have done honor to Don Quixote.

"If you fight them and whip them, they will waylay you and kill you. But there are ten of them, and if you fight them you will be killed, and this lady will be without a protector. If you run away, the house will be destroyed, and you will be killed whenever you are found. But what have you here—a magic lantern?"

The old gentleman had, before Edwards's arrival, taken down the instrument to introduce some improvement which he had just invented. When Edwards stumbled over it and called it a magic lantern he looked at him scornfully.

"A magic lantern!" he cried. "No, sir; that is a dissolving view, oxy-calcium, panto-sciostereoscopticon."

"With this we must save you and your daughter from the half-breeds," said the trapper, a little impatient at this ill-timed manifestation of pedantry. "Get ready for action immediately."

"I have no oxygen gas."

"Make it at once," said Edwards. He picked up some papers marked "chlor. potass." and "black oxide."

"Here is your material," he said.

"Do you understand chemistry?" asked Lindsley. But the trapper did not answer. He got out the retort, and in five minutes the oxygen was bubbling furiously through the wash bottle into the India-rubber receiver. Edwards stood at the window scanning the

64

road toward Gager's with his telescope until it grew dark, which in that latitude was at about ten o'clock. Then the magic lantern was removed to the little grass-roofed stable, in which dwelt a solitary pony, and by Edwards's direction the focus was carefully set so that it would throw a picture against the house. Edwards selected two pictures and adjusted them for use in the two tubes.

The half-breeds were not in haste, and in all the long hour of suspense Emilia, hidden in the barn with her father and young Edwards, was positively happy. For here was human companionship, and a hungry soul will gladly risk death if by that means companionship can be purchased. It did not matter either that conversation was out of the question. It is presence, and not talk, that makes companionship.

But hark! the bois brûlés are on the bank of the river below. Emilia's heart grew still as she heard them swear. Their sacr-r-r-ré rolled like the rattle of a rattlesnake. They were coming up the hill, quarreling drunkenly about the powder. Now they were between the house and the stable, getting ready to dig a hole for the "poudre à canon"

"I'll give them fireworks!" said Edwards in a whisper.

A picture of Thorwaldsen's bas-relief of "Morning" having been previously placed in the instrument, Edwards now removed the cap, and the beautiful flying female figure, with the infant in her arms, shone out upon the side of the house with marvelous vividness.

"By thunder!" said Whisky Jim, steadying himself, while every hair stood on end.

"Mon Dieu!" cried the bois brûlés, who had never seen a picture in their lives except in the cathedral of St. Boniface, at Fort Garry. "Mon Dieu! La Sainte Vierge!" And they fell on their knees before this apparition of the Blessed Virgin, and crossed themselves and prayed lustily.

But "Whisky Jim" straightened himself up, and hiccoughed, and stammered "By thunder!" and added some words which, being Saxon, I will not print.

"The devil!" cried Jim, a minute later, starting down the hill at

65

full speed, for, by Edwards's direction, the light had been shifted to the other tube in such a way as to dissolve the "Morning" into a hideous picture of the conventional horned and hoofed devil. The picture was originally meant to be comic, but it now set Jim to running for dear life.

"Oui, c'est le diable! le diable! le diable!" cried the frantic bois brûlés, breaking off their invocations to the Virgin most abruptly, and fleeing pellmell down the hill after Jim, falling over one another as they ran. Quick as a flash Edwards threw about him a sheet which he had ready, and pursued the fleeing Frenchmen. Jim had already seized the reins, and, on the plan of "the devil take the hindmost," was driving at a pace that would have done him credit in the Central Park, up the trail toward Gager's, leaving the half-breeds to get on as best they could. Bourdon stumbled and fell, and Edwards lavished some blows upon him that must have satisfied the bois brûlé that ghosts have a most solid corporeal existence.

Then Edwards returned and captured the keg of powder. He assured the Lindsleys that the superstitious half-breeds would never again venture within five miles of a house that was guarded by the Holy Virgin and the devil in partnership. And they never did. Even the Indians were afraid to approach the place, pronouncing it "Wakan," or supernaturally inhabited. They regarded Lindsley as a "medicine-man" of great power.

But what a night that was! For Edwards stayed two hours, and made the acquaintance of Lindsley and his daughter. And how he talked, while Emilia thought she had never known how heaven felt before; and the old man forgot his inventions, and did not broach more than twenty of his theories in the two hours. He was so much interested in the tall trapper that he forgot the rest. Edwards ate a supper set out by the hands of Emilia, and left at three o'clock. He was at Pelican Lake next morning, and no man suspected his share in the affair except Gager, who had sense enough to say nothing. And Emilia lay down and dreamed of angels about the house. One was like Thorwaldsen's "Morning," and the other wore long hair and beard, and was very tall.

This abortive attempt to make a skyrocket out of Lindsley's

cabin wrought only good to Emilia at first. The father was now wholly in love with the trapper. He praised him at all hours.

"He is a philosopher, my daughter. He understands chemistry. He lives in the arcana of nature and reads her secrets. No foolish study of the heathen classics; no training after mediæval fashion in one of our colleges, which are anachronisms, has perverted his taste. Here is the Émile worthy of my Emilia," he would say, much to the daughter's annoyance.

But when Edwards came the hours were golden. Hanging his wolf-skin cap behind the door, and shaking back his long locks as he took his seat, he would entrance father and daughter alike with his talk of adventure. From the time of his first visit new life came to the heart of Emilia; and Mr. Lindsley, whose every whim the trapper humored, was as much fascinated as his daughter. But now commenced a fierce battle in the heart of Emilia. Edwards loved her. By all the speech that his eyes were capable of, he told her so. And by all the beating of her own heart she knew that she loved the brown-faced, long-haired trapper in return. But what about the fair-eyed student, who for very love and disappointment had gone to the arctic seas? He was not at hand to plead his cause, and for this very reason her conscience pleaded it for him. When her soul had fed on the words of the trapper as upon manna in the wilderness, she took up the old photograph and the eyes reproached her. She shed bitter tears of penitence upon it for her disloyalty to the storm-tossed sailor, but rejoiced again when she saw the tall figure of the trapper coming down the trail. A desolate and lonely heart can not live forever on the memory of a dead love. And have ye not read what David did when he was an hungered? Do not, therefore, reproach a starving soul for partaking of this feast in the desert.

And so Emilia tried to believe that Brown was long since dead—poor fellow! She shed tears over an imaginary grave in Labrador with a great sense of comfort. She tried to think that he had long since married and forgotten her, and she endeavored to nurse some feeble pangs of jealousy toward an imaginary wife.

Now it was very improper, doubtless, in Brown to come to life just at this moment. One lover too many is as destructive to the happiness of a conscientious girl as one too few. If Emilia had been trained in society, her joy at having two lovers would have had no alloy save her grief that there were not four of them. But it was one of the misfortunes of her solitary and peculiar education that she had conscience and maidenly modesty. Wherefore it was a source of bitter distress and embarrassment to her that, at the end of a long letter from a neighbor who had taken a notion after years of silence to write her all the gossip of the old village, she found these words: "Your old friend Brown did not jump into the sea at grief for his rejection, after all. He has written to somebody here that he is coming home. I believe he said that he loved you all the same as ever."

The greatest grief of Emilia was that she should have been so wicked as to be grieved. Had she not prayed all these years, when she could pray at all, for the safety of the young student? Had she not prayed against storms and icebergs? And now that he was coming, her heart smote her as if he were a ghost of some one whom she had murdered! Whether she loved him, or Edwards, or anybody, indeed she could not tell. But she would do penance for her crime. And so, when next she heard the quiet voice of "the long trapper" asking for her, she refused to see him, though the refusal all but killed her.

Poor Edwards! How he paced the shore of Swan Lake all that night! For when love comes into the soul of a solitary man it has all the force that all the thousand interests of life have to one in the busy world. How terrible were the temptations that sometimes assailed the religious eremites we can never guess.

Sunset of the next day found Edwards in the Red River Valley, far on his way toward Fort Garry, bent on spending the rest of his life as a "free trader" in British America. As for Emilia, she was now in total darkness. The sun had set, and the moon had not appeared. Brown might be dead, or she might not love him, or he might never find her. And she had thrown away her paradise, and there was only blackness left.

Edwards had already come within a few miles of Georgetown, where he was to take passage in that strangest of all the craft that ever frightened away the elk, the little seven-by-nine steamer Anson Northrup, when, as he was striding desperately along the trail, he was suddenly checked by a thought. He stood five minutes in indecision, then turned and began to walk rapidly in the opposite direction. At Breckinridge he found a stage, and getting out at Gager's he went down the trail toward Lindsley's.

Now Davy Lindsley had been in a terrible state of ferment. When he had found the philosopher, "the uncontaminated child of Nature, the self-educated combination of civilized and savage man," his daughter had perversely refused him, and the old man had taken the disappointment so to heart that he was in a state bordering on frenzy.

"Misfortune always pursues me!" he began, when he met Edwards under the hill. "Fifty times I have been near achieving some great result, and my ill luck has spoiled it all. You see me a broken-hearted man. To have allied my family with a child of Nature like yourself would have given me the greatest joy. But—how shall I express my grief?" And here the old man struck a pathetically tragic attitude and drew out his handkerchief, weeping with a profound self-pity.

"Mr. Lindsley, do you know why Miss Lindsley has become so suddenly displeased with me?" asked the trapper, trembling.

"Miss Lindsley, sir, is perverse. It is the one evil trait that my enlightened system of education, drawn from Rousseau, Pestalozzi, Froebel, and Herbert Spencer, and combined by my own genius—it is the one evil trait that my system has failed to eradicate. She is perverse. I fear, sir, she is yet worshiping the image of a misguided youth who, filled and puffed up with the useless learning of the schools, ventured to address her. I am the most unfortunate of men."

"Mr. Lindsley, can I see your daughter alone?"

The old man thought he could. But she was very perverse. In truth, that very morning Emilia had, in a sublime spirit of self-immolation, vowed that she would love none but the long-lost lover, and that if Brown never came back she would die heroically devoted to him, and thus she had sacrificed to her conscience and it

69

was appeased. But right atop this vow came the request of Edwards for an interview. Was ever a girl so beset? Could she trust herself? On thinking it over she was afraid not; so that it was only by much persuasion that she was prevailed on to grant the request.

While Edwards talked she could but listen, frightened all the time at the faintness of her solemn resolution, which had seemed so irrevocable when she made it. He frankly demanded the reason for her change of conduct toward him. And she, like an honest and simple-hearted girl, told the other love story with a trembling voice, while Edwards listened with eyes downcast.

"This was five years ago?" he asked.

"Yes, sir."

"And the young man's name?"

"Was Edward Brown."

"Curious! I think," he said slowly, pausing as if to get breath and keep his self-control, "I think, if my hair were cut off short and parted on one side as Edward Brown wore his, instead of in the middle, and if my whiskers were shaven off, and if the tan of five years' exposure were gone from my face, and if I were five years younger, and two inches shorter, I think— —" He paused here and looked at her.

"Please say the rest quickly," she said in a faint whisper. For the setting sun was streaming in at the west window upon the face of the trapper. His hair was thrown back, and he was looking into her eyes with a look she had never seen before. But he dropped his head upon his hand now and looked at the floor.

"It might be," he spoke musingly, "it might be that Edward Brown failed to reach his ship in time at New Bedford, and changed his mind and came here, and that after Emilia came he watched this house day and night till his heart came nigh to bursting. But I was going to say," he said, rousing himself, "that in case the years and the tan and the hair could be taken off, and this trapper coat changed into one of finer cut and material, and the name reversed, that Browne Edwards, the trapper, would be nearer of kin than a twin brother to Edward Brown, the broken-hearted student."

What Emilia did just here I do not know, and if I did I should not tell you. To faint would have been the proper thing. But, poor girl! her education had been neglected, and I think she did not faint. When the old philosopher came in he was charmed with the situation, and that evening, when they two walked together on the bank of the Pomme de Terre, Emilia pointed to the stars, and said: "Do you know that in all these years God has seemed to me a cruel monster turning a crank? And to-night every star seems to be an eye through which God is looking at me, as my mother used to. I feel as though God were loving me. See, the stars are laughing in my face! Now I love Him as I did my mother. And to-night I am going to read that curious story about Christ at the wedding."

For God, who is love, loves to find his way to a human heart through love. And Edwards, who had been in bitterness and rebellion during the years of his exile, listened now to the voice of love as to that of an angel whom God had sent out of heaven to bring him back home again.

Mr. Lindsley is an invalid now. Lindsleyville belongs to Browne Edwards and his wife. And old Davy has made a will on twenty quires of legal cap, bequeathing to his son-in-law all his right, title, and interest in certain and sundry patents on churns, cannons, beehives, magic lanterns, flying machines, etc., together with some extraordinary secret discoveries. The old gentleman is slowly dying in the full conviction that he is bequeathing the foundation of an immense fortune to his son-in-law, and more wisdom to the world than has been contributed to its stock by all that have gone before. And he often reminds Emilia that she has to thank him for getting so good a husband. If it hadn't been for him she might have married that sickly student.

1871

THE STORY OF A VALENTINE

When my friend Capt. Terrible, U.S.N., dines at my plain table, I am a little abashed. I know that he has been accustomed always to a variety of wines and sauces, to a cigarette after each course, and to cookery that would kill an undeveloped American. So, when the captain turns the castor round three times before selecting his condiment, and when his eyes seem to be seeking for Worcestershire sauce and Burgundy wine, I feel the poverty of the best feast I can furnish him. I am afraid veteran magazine readers will feel thus about the odd little story I have to tell. For I have observed of late that even the short stories are highly seasoned; and I can not bear to disappoint readers. So, let me just honestly write over the gateway to this story a warning. I have no Cayenne pepper. No Worcestershire sauce. No cognac. No cigarettes. No murders. No suicides. No broken hearts. No lovers' quarrels. No angry father. No pistols and coffee. No arsenic. No laudanum. No shrewd detectives. No trial for murder. No "heartless coquette." No "deep-dyed villain with a curling mustache." Now if, after this warning, you have the courage to go on, I am not responsible.

Hubert said I might print it if I would disguise the names. It came out quite incidentally. We were discussing the woman question. I am a "woman's righter." Hubert—the Rev. Hubert Lee, I should say, pastor of the "First Church," and, indeed, the only church in Allenville—is not, though I flatter myself I have made some impression on him. But the discussion took place in Hubert's own house, and wishing to give a pleasant turn at the end, I suppose, he told me how, a year and a half before, he had "used up" one woman's-rights man, who was no other than old Dr. Hood, the physician that has had charge of the physical health of Hubert and myself from the beginning. Unlike most of his profession, the doctor has always been a radical, and even the wealth that has come in upon him of late years has left him quite as much of a radical, at least in theory, as ever. Indeed, the old doctor is not very inconsistent in practice, for he has educated his only daughter,

72

Cornelia, to his own profession, and I believe she took her M.D. with honors, though she has lately spoiled her prospects by marrying. But socially he has become a little aristocratic, seeking an exclusive association with his wealthy neighbors. And this does not look very well in one who, when he was poor, was particularly bitter on "a purse-proud aristocracy." I suppose Hubert felt this. Certainly I did, and therefore I enjoyed the conversation that he repeated to me all the more.

It seems that my friend Hubert had been away at the seminary for three years, and that having at last conquered in his great battle against poverty, and having gained an education in spite of difficulties, and having supplied a city church acceptably for some months during the absence of the pastor in Europe, he came back to our native village to rest on his laurels a few weeks, and to decide which of three rather impecunious calls he would accept. When just about to leave he took it into his head, for some reason, to "drop in" on old Doctor Hood. It was nine o'clock in the morning, and the doctor's partner was making morning calls, while the old gentleman sat in his office to attend to any that might seek his services. This particular morning happened to be an unfortunate one, for there were no ague-shaken patients to be seen, and there was not even a case of minor surgery to relieve the tediousness of the morning office hour. Perhaps it was for this reason, perhaps it was for the sake of old acquaintance, that he gave Hubert a most cordial reception, and launched at once into a sea of vivacious talk. Cornelia, who was in the office, excused herself on the ground that she was cramming for her final examination, and seated herself at a window with her book.

"I am afraid I take your time, doctor," said Hubert.

"Oh, no, I am giving up practice to my partner, Dr. Beck, and shall give it all to him in a year or two."

"To him and Miss Cornelia?" queried Hubert, laughing. For it was currently reported that the young doctor and Cornelia were to form a partnership in other than professional affairs.

Either because he wished to attract her attention, or for some other reason, Hubert soon managed to turn the conversation to the subject of woman's rights, and the old doctor and the young parson were soon hurling at each other all the staple and now somewhat stale arguments about woman's fitness and woman's unfitness for many things. At last, perhaps because he was a little cornered, Hubert said:

"Now, doctor, there was a queer thing happened to a student in my class in the seminary. I don't suppose, doctor, that you are much interested in a love story, but I would just like to tell you this one, because I think you dare not apply your principles to it in every part. Theories often fail when practically applied, you know."

"Go on, Hu, go on; I'd like to hear the story. And as for my principles, they'll bear applying anywhere!" and the old doctor rubbed his hands together confidently.

"This friend of mine, Henry Gilbert," said Hu, "was, like myself, poor. A long time ago, when he was a boy, the son of a poor widow, the lot on which he lived joined at the back the lot on which lived a Mr. Morton, at that time a thriving merchant, now the principal capitalist in that part of the country. As there was a back gate between the lots, my friend was the constant playmate from earliest childhood of Jennie Morton. He built her playhouses out of old boards, he molded clay bricks for her use, and carved tiny toys out of pine blocks for her amusement. As he grew larger, and as Jennie's father grew richer and came to live in greater style, Henry grew more shy. But by all the unspoken language of the eyes the two never failed to make their unchanging regard known to each other.

"Henry went to college early. At vacation time the two met. But the growing difference in their social position could not but be felt. Jennie's friends were of a different race from his own. Her parents never thought of inviting him to their entertainments. And if they had, a rusty coat and a lack of money to spend on kid gloves would have effectually kept him away. He was proud. This apparent neglect stung him. It is true that Jennie Morton was all the more kind. But his quick and foolish pride made him fancy that he detected pity in her kindness. And yet all this only made him determined to place himself in a position in which he could ask her

74

hand as her equal. But you do not understand, doctor, as I do, how irresistible is this conviction of duty in regard to the ministry. Under that pressure my friend settled it that he must preach. And now there was before him a good ten years of poverty at least. What should he do about it?

"In his extremity he took advice of a favorite theological professor. The professor advised him not to seek the hand of a rich girl. She would not be suited to the trials of a minister's life. But finding that Henry was firm in his opinion that this sound general principle did not in the least apply to this particular case, the professor proceeded to touch the tenderest chord in the young man's heart. He told him that it would be ungenerous, and in some sense dishonorable, for him to take a woman delicately brought up into the poverty and trial incident to a minister's life. If you understood, sir, how morbid his sense of honor is, you would not wonder at the impression this suggestion made upon him. To give up the ministry was in his mind to be a traitor to duty and to God. To win her, if he could, was to treat ungenerously her whose happiness was dearer to him a thousand times than his own."

"I hope he did not give her up," said the doctor.

"Yes, he gave her up, in a double spirit of mediæval self-sacrifice. Looking toward the ministry, he surrendered his love as some of the old monks sacrificed love, ambition, and all other things to conscience. Looking at her happiness, he sacrificed his hopes in a more than knightly devotion to her welfare. The knights sometimes gave their lives. He gave more.

"For three years he did not trust himself to return to his home. But, having graduated and settled himself for nine months over a church, there was no reason why he shouldn't go to see his mother again; and once in the village, the sight of the old schoolhouse and the old church revived a thousand memories that he had been endeavoring to banish. The garden walks, and especially the apple trees, that are the most unchangeable of landmarks, revived the old passion with undiminished power. He paced his room at night. He looked out at the new house of his rich neighbor. He chafed under the restraint of his vow not to think again of Jennie Morton. It was the old story of the monk who thinks the world subdued, but who finds it all at once about to assume the mastery of him. I do not know how the struggle might have ended, but it was all at once stopped from without.

"There reached him a rumor that Jennie was already the betrothed wife of a Colonel Pearson, who was her father's partner in business. And, indeed, Colonel Pearson went in and out at Mr. Morton's gate every evening, and the father was known to favor his suit.

"Jennie was not engaged to him, however. Three times she had refused him. The fourth time, in deference to her father's wishes, she had consented to 'think about it' for a week. In truth, Henry had been at home ten days and had not called upon her, and all the hope she had cherished in that direction, and all the weary waiting, seemed in vain. When the colonel's week was nearly out she heard that Henry was to leave in two days. In a sort of desperation she determined to accept Colonel Pearson without waiting for the time appointed for her answer. But that gentleman spoiled it all by his own overconfidence.

"For when he called, after Jennie had determined on this course, he found her so full of kindness that he hardly knew how to behave with moderation. And so he fell to flattering her, and flattering himself at the same time that he knew all the ins and outs of a girl's heart, he complimented her on the many offers she had received.

"'And I tell you what,' he proceeded, 'there are plenty of others that would lay their heads at your feet if they were only your equals. There's that young parson—Gilbert, I think they call him— that is visiting his mother in the unpainted and threadbare-looking little house that stands behind this one. I've actually seen that fellow, in his rusty, musty coat, stop and look after you on the street; and every night, when I go home, he is sitting at the window that looks over this way. The poor fool is in love with you. Only think of it! And I chuckle to myself when I see him, and say, "Don't you wish you could reach so high?" I declare, it's funny.'

"In that one speech Colonel Pearson dashed his chances to

76

pieces. He could not account for the sudden return of winter in Jennie Morton's manner. And all his sunshine was powerless to dispel it, or to bring back the least approach of spring.

"Poor Jennie! You can imagine, doctor, how she paced the floor all that night. She began to understand something of the courage of Henry Gilbert's heart, and something of the manliness of his motives. All night long she watched the light burning in the room in the widow's house; and all night long she debated the matter until her head ached. She could reach but one conclusion: Henry was to leave the day after to-morrow. If any communication should ever be opened between them she must begin it. It was as if she had seen him drifting away from her forever, and must throw him a rope. I think even such a woman's-right man as yourself would hardly justify her, however, in taking any step of the kind."

"I certainly should," said the doctor.

"But she could not find a way—she had no rope to throw. Again the colonel, meaning to do anything else but that, opened the way. At the breakfast table the next morning she received from him a magnificent valentine. All at once she saw her method. It was St. Valentine's day. The rope was in her hand. Excusing herself from breakfast she hastened to her room.

"To send a valentine to the faithful lover was the uppermost thought. But how? She dare not write her name, for, after all, she might be mistaken in counting on his love, or she might offend his prejudices or his pride by so direct an approach. She went fumbling in a drawer for stationery. She drew out a little pine boat that Henry had whittled for her many years before. He had named it 'Hope,' but the combined wisdom of the little boy and girl could not succeed in spelling the name correctly. And here was the little old boat that he had given, saying often afterward that it was the boat they two were going to sail in some day. The misspelt name had been the subject of many a laugh between them. Now—but I mustn't be sentimental.

"It did not take Jennie long to draw an exact likeness of the little craft. And that there might be no mistake about it, she spelled the name as it was on the side of the boat:

77

"There was not another word in the valentine. Sealing it up, she hurried out with it and dropped it in the post office. No merchant, sending all his fortune to sea in one frail bark, ever watched the departure and trembled for the result of venture as she did. Spain did not pray half so fervently when the invincible armada sailed. It was an unuttered prayer—an unutterable prayer. For heart and hope were the lading of the little picture boat that sailed out that day, with no wind but her wishes in its sails.

"She sat down at her window until she saw Henry Gilbert pass the next street corner on his morning walk to the post office. Three minutes after, he went home, evidently in a great state of excitement, with her valentine open in his hand. After a while he went back again toward the post office, and returned. Had he taken a reply?

"Jennie again sought the office. There were people all around, with those hideous things that they call comic valentines open in their hands. And they actually seemed to think them funny! She had a reply. It did not take her long to find her room and to open it. There was another picture of a boat, but the name on its side read 'Despair.' And these words were added: 'Your boat is the pleasantest, but understanding that there was no vacant place upon it, I have been obliged to take passage on this.' Slowly the meaning forced itself upon her. Henry had fears that she whom he thought engaged was coqueting with him. I think, doctor, you will hardly justify her in proceeding further with the correspondence?"

"Why not? Hasn't a woman as much right to make herself understood in such a matter as a man? And when the social advantages are on her side the burden of making the advances often falls upon her. Many women do it indirectly and are not censured."

"Well, you know I'm conservative, doctor, but I'm glad you're consistent. She did send another valentine. I am afraid she strained this figure of speech about the boat. But when everything in the world depends on one metaphor, it will not do to be fastidious.

78

Jennie drew again the little boat with misspelt name. And this time she added five words: 'The master's place is vacant.'

"And quite late in the afternoon the reply was left at the door: 'I am an applicant for the vacant place, if you will take that of master's maté.'"

"Good!" cried the doctor; "I always advocated giving women every liberty in these matters."

"But I will stump you yet, doctor," said Hubert. "That evening Gough was to lecture in the village, and my friend went not to hear Gough but to see Miss Jennie Morton at a distance. Somehow in the stupefaction of revived hope he had not thought of going to the house to see her yet. He had postponed his departure and had thrown away his scruples. Knowing how much opposition he would have to contend with, he thought—if he thought at all—that he must proceed with caution. But some time after the lecture began he discovered the Morton family without Jennie! Slowly it all dawned upon him. She was at home waiting for him. He was near the front of the church in which the lecture was held, and every inch of aisle was full of people. To get out was not easy. But as he thought of Jennie waiting, it became a matter of life and death. If the house had been on fire he would not have been more intent on making his exit. He reached the door, he passed the happiest evening of his life, only to awake to sorrow, for Jennie's father is 'dead set' against the match."

"He has no right to interfere," said the doctor vehemently. "You see, I stand by my principles."

"But if I tell the story out I am afraid you would not," said Hubert.

"Why, isn't it done?"

"I beg your pardon, doctor, for having used a little craft. I had much at stake. I have disguised this story in its details. But it is true, I am the hero——"

The doctor looked quickly towards his daughter. Her head was bent low over her book. Her long hair hung about it like a curtain, shutting out all view of the face. The doctor walked to the other window and looked out. Hubert sat like a mummy. After a minute Dr. Hood spoke.

79

"Cornelia!"

She lifted a face that was aflame. Tears glistened in her eyes, and I doubt not there was a prayer in her heart.

"You are a brave girl. I had other plans. You have a right to choose for yourself. God bless you both! But it's a great pity Hu is not a lawyer; he pleads well." So saying he put on his hat and walked out.

This is the conversation that Hubert repeated to me that day sitting in his own little parsonage in Allenville. A minute after his wife came in. She had been prescribing for the minor ailments of some poor neighbors. She took the baby from her crib, and bent over her till that same long hair curtained mother and child from sight.

"I think," said Hubert, "that you folks who write love stories make a great mistake in stopping at marriage. The honeymoon never truly begins until conjugal affection is enriched by this holy partnership of loving hearts in the life of a child. The climax of a love story is not the wedding. It is the baby!"

"What do you call her?" I asked.

"Hope," said the mother.

"Hope Valentine," added the father, with a significant smile.

"And you spell the Hope with an 'a,' I believe," I said.

"You naughty Hu!" said Mrs. Cornelia. "You've been telling. You think that love story is interesting to others because you enjoy it so much!"

1871

HULDAH, THE HELP[2]

A THANKSGIVING LOVE STORY

I remember a story that Judge Balcom told a few years ago on the afternoon of Thanksgiving Day. I do not feel sure that it will interest everybody as it did me. Indeed, I am afraid that it will not, and yet I can not help thinking that it is just the sort of a trifle that will go well with turkey, celery, and mince pie.

It was in the judge's own mansion on Thirty-fourth Street that I heard it. It does not matter to the reader how I, a stranger, came to be one of that family party. Since I could not enjoy the society of my own family, it was an act of Christian charity that permitted me to share the joy of others. We had eaten dinner and had adjourned to the warm, bright parlor. I have noticed on such occasions that conversation is apt to flag after dinner. Whether it is that digestion absorbs all of one's vitality, or for some other reason, at least so it generally falls out, that people may talk ever so brilliantly at the table, but they will hardly keep it up for the first half-hour afterward. And so it happened that some of the party fell to looking at the books, and some to turning the leaves of the photograph album, while others were using the stereoscope. For my own part, I was staring at an engraving in a dark corner of the parlor, where I could not have made out much of its purpose if I had desired, but in reality I was thinking of the joyous company of my own kith and kin, hundreds of miles away, and regretting that I could not be with them.

---

[2] This is the first story written by me, beyond a few juvenile tales; and it was the first short story to appear in Scribner's Monthly, the present Century Magazine. Mr. Gilder, then associated with Dr. Holland in editing that newborn periodical, begged me to write a short story for the second number of the magazine. I told him that something Helps had written suggested that a story might be devised in which the hero should marry a servant. He said it couldn't be done, and I wrote this, on a wager, as it were. But a "help" is not a servant. The popularity of this story encouraged me to continue, but I can not now account for the popularity of the story.

"What are you thinking about, papa?" asked Irene, the judge's second daughter.

She was a rather haughty-looking girl of sixteen, but, as I had noticed, very much devoted to her parents. At this moment she was running her hand through her father's hair, while he was rousing himself from his revery to answer her question.

"Thinking of the old Thanksgivings, which were so different from anything we have here. They were the genuine thing; these are only counterfeits."

"Come, tell us about them, please." This time it was Annie Balcom, the elder girl, who spoke. And we all gathered round the judge. For I notice that when conversation does revive, after that period of silence that follows dinner, it is very attractive to the whole company, and in whatsoever place it breaks out there is soon a knot of interested listeners.

"I don't just now think of any particular story of New England Thanksgivings that would interest you," said the judge.

"Tell them about Huldah's mince pie," said Mrs. Balcom, as she looked up from a copy of Whittier she had been reading.

I can not pretend to give the story which follows exactly in the judge's words, for it is three years since I heard it, but as nearly as I can remember it was as follows:

There was a young lawyer named John Harlow practicing law here in New York twenty odd years ago. His father lived not very far from my father. John had been graduated with honors, had studied law, and had the good fortune to enter immediately into a partnership with his law preceptor, ex-Gov. Blank. So eagerly had he pursued his studies that for two years he had not seen his country home. I think one reason why he had not cared to visit it was that his mother was dead, and his only sister was married and living in Boston. Take the "women folks" out of a house, and it never seems much like home to a young man.

But now, as Thanksgiving day drew near, he resolved to give himself a brief release from the bondage of books. He told his partner that he wanted to go home for a week. He said he wanted to see his father and the boys, and his sister, who was coming home

82

at that time, but that he specially wanted to ride old Bob to the brook once more, and to milk Cherry again, just to see how it felt to be a farmer's boy.

"John," said the old lawyer, "be sure you fix up a match with some of those country girls. No man is fit for anything till he is well married; and you are now able, with economy, to support a wife. Mind you get one of those country girls. These paste and powder people here aren't fit for a young man who wants a woman."

"Governor," said the young lawyer, laying his boots gracefully up on top of a pile of law books, as if to encourage reflection by giving his head the advantage of the lower end of the inclined plane, "Governor, I don't know anything about city girls. I have given myself to my books. But I must have a wife that is literary, like myself—one that can understand Emerson, for instance."

The old lawyer laughed. "John," he answered, "the worst mistake you can make is to marry a woman just like yourself in taste. You don't want to marry a woman's head, but her heart."

John defended his theory, and the governor only remarked that he would be cured of that sooner or later, and the sooner the better.

The next morning John had a letter from his sister. Part of it ran about thus:

"I've concluded, old fellow, that if you don't marry you'll dry up and turn to parchment. I'm going to bring home with me the smartest girl I know. She reads Carlyle, and quotes Goethe, and understands Emerson. Of course she don't know what I am up to, but you must prepare to capitulate."

John did not like Amanda's assuming to pick a wife for him, but he did like the prospect of meeting a clever girl, and he opened the letter again to make sure that he had not misunderstood. He read again, "understands Emerson." John was pleased. Why? I think I can divine. John was vain of his own abilities, and he wanted a woman that could appreciate him. He would have told you that he wanted congenial society. But congenial female society to an ambitious man whose heart is yet untouched is only society that, in some sense, understands his greatness and admires his wisdom.

In the old home they were looking for the son. The family proper consisted of the father, good Deacon Harlow, John's two brothers, ten and twelve years old, and Huldah, the "help." This last was the daughter of a neighboring farmer who was poor and hopelessly rheumatic, and most of the daughter's hard earnings went to eke out the scanty subsistence at home. Aunt Judith, the sister of John's mother, "looked after" the household affairs of her brother-in-law, by coming over once a week and helping Huldah darn and mend and make, and by giving Huldah such advice as her inexperience was supposed to require. But now Deacon Harlow's daughter had left her husband to eat his turkey alone in Boston, and had brought her two children home to receive the paternal blessing. Not that Mrs. Amanda Holmes had the paternal blessing chiefly in view in her trip. She had brought with her a very dear friend, Miss Janet Dunton, the accomplished teacher in the Mount Parnassus Female Seminary. Why Miss Janet Dunton came to the country with her friend she could hardly have told. Not a word had Mrs. Holmes spoken to her on the subject of the matrimonial scheme. She would have resented any allusion to such a project. She would have repelled any insinuation that she had ever dreamed that marriage was desirable under any conceivable circumstances. It is a way we have of teaching girls to lie. We educate them to catch husbands. Every superadded accomplishment is put on with the distinct understanding that its sole use is to make the goods more marketable. We get up parties, we go to watering places, we buy dresses, we refurnish our houses, to help our girls to a good match. And then we teach them to abhor the awful wickedness of ever confessing the great desire that nature and education have combined to make the chief longing of their hearts. We train them to lie to us, their trainers; we train them to lie to themselves; to be false with everybody on this subject; to say "no" when they mean "yes"; to deny an engagement when they are dying to boast of it. It is one of the refinements of Christian civilization which we pray the Women's Missionary Society not to communicate to poor ignorant heathens who know no better than to tell the truth about these things.

84

But, before I digressed into that line of remark, I was saying that Miss Janet Dunton would have resented the most remote suggestion of marriage. She often declared sentimentally that she was wedded to her books, and loved her leisure, and was determined to be an old maid. And all the time this sincere Christian girl was dying to confer herself upon some worthy man of congenial tastes; which meant, in her case, just what it did in John Harlow's—some one who could admire her attainments. But, sensitive as she was to any imputation of a desire to marry, she and Mrs. Holmes understood each other distinctly. There is a freemasonry of women, and these two had made signs. They had talked about in this wise:

Mrs. Holmes.—My dear Janet, you'll find my brother a bear in manners, I fear. I wish he would marry. I hope you won't break his heart, for I know you wouldn't have him.

Miss Dunton.—You know my views on that subject, my dear. I love books, and shall marry nobody. Besides, your brother's great legal and literary attainments would frighten such a poor little mouse as I am.

And in saying those words they had managed to say that John Harlow was an unsophisticated student, and that they would run him down between them.

Mrs. Holmes and her friend had arrived twenty-four hours ahead of John, and the daughter of the house had already installed herself as temporary mistress by thoughtlessly upsetting, reversing, and turning inside out all the good Huldah's most cherished arrangements. All the plans for the annual festival that wise and practical Huldah had entertained were vetoed, without a thought that this young girl had been for a year and a half in actual authority in the house, and might have some feeling of wrong in having a guest of a week overturn her plans for the next month. But Mrs. Holmes was not one of the kind to think of that. Huldah was hired and paid, and she never dreamed that hired people could have any interests in their work or their home other than their pay and their food. But Huldah was patient, though she confessed that she had a feeling that she had been rudely "trampled all over." I suspect she had a good cry at the end of the first day. I can not affirm it, except from a general knowledge of women.

When John drove up in the buggy that the boys had taken to the depot for him his first care was to shake hands with the deacon, who was glad to see him, but could not forbear expressing a hope that he would "shave that hair off his upper lip." Then John greeted his sister cordially, and was presented to Miss Dunton. Instead of sitting down, he pushed right on into the kitchen, where Huldah, in a calico frock and a clean white apron, was baking biscuit for tea. She had been a schoolmate of his, and he took her hand cordially as she stood there, with the bright western sun half-glorifying her head and face.

"Why, Huldah, how you've grown!" was his first word of greeting. He meant more than he said, for, though she was not handsome, she had grown exceeding comely as she developed into a woman.

"Undignified as ever!" said Amanda, as he returned to the sitting room.

"How?" said John. He looked bewildered. What had he done that was undignified? And Amanda Holmes saw well enough that it would not do to tell him that speaking to Huldah Manners was not consistent with dignity. She saw that her remark had been a mistake, and she got out of it as best she could by turning the conversation. Several times during the supper John addressed his conversation to Huldah, who sat at the table with the family; for in the country in those days it would have been considered a great outrage to make a "help" wait for the second table. John would turn from the literary conversation to inquire of Huldah about his old playmates, some of whom had gone to the West, some of whom had died, and some of whom were settling into the same fixed adherence to their native rocks that had characterized their ancestors.

The next day the ladies could get no good out of John Harlow. He got up early and milked the cow. He cut wood and carried it in for Huldah. He rode old Bob to the brook for water. He

86

did everything that he had been accustomed to do when a boy, finding as much pleasure in forgetting that he was a man as he had once found in hoping to be a man. The two boys enjoyed his society greatly, and his father was delighted to see that he had retained his interest in the farm life, though the deacon evidently felt an unconquerable hostility to what he called "that scrub-brush on the upper lip." I think if John had known how strong his father's feeling was against this much cherished product he would have mowed the crop and grazed the field closely until he got back to the city.

John was not insensible to Janet Dunton's charms. She could talk fluently about all the authors most in vogue, and the effect of her fluency was really dazzling to a man not yet cultivated enough himself to see how superficial her culture was; for all her learning floated on top. None of it had influenced her own culture. She was brim full of that which she had acquired, but it had not been incorporated into her own nature. John did not see this, and he was infatuated with the idea of marrying a wife of such attainments. How she would dazzle his friends! How the governor would like to talk to her! How she would shine in his parlors! How she would delight people as she gave them tea and talk at the same time. John was in love with her as he would have been in love with a new tea urn or a rare book. She was a nice thing to show. Other people than John have married on the strength of such a feeling and called it love; for John really imagined that he was in love. And during that week he talked and walked and rode in the sleigh with Miss Dunton, and had made up his mind that he would carry this brilliant prize to New York. But, with lawyerlike caution, he thought he would put off the committal as long as possible. If his heart had been in his attentions the caution would not have been worth much. Caution is a good breakwater against vanity, but it isn't worth much against the springtide of love, as John Harlow soon found out.

For toward the end of the week he began to feel a warmer feeling for Miss Janet. It was not in the nature of things that John should walk and talk with a pleasant girl a week, and not feel something more than his first interested desire to marry a showy wife. His heart began to be touched, and he resolved to bring things to a crisis as soon as possible. He therefore sought an opportunity to propose. But it was hard to find. For though Mrs. Holmes was tolerably ingenious, she could not get the boys or the deacon to pay any regard to her hints. Boys are totally depraved on such questions anyhow, and always manage to stumble in where any privacy is sought. And as for the deacon, it really seemed as though he had some design in intruding at the critical moment.

I do not think that John was seriously in love with Miss Dunton. If he had been he would have found some means of communicating with her. A thousand spies with sleepless eyes all round their heads can not keep a man from telling his love somehow, if he really have a love to tell.

There is another fact which convinces me that John Harlow was not yet very deeply in love with Janet. He was fond of talking with her of Byron and Milton, of Lord Bacon and Emerson—i.e., as I have already said, he was fond of putting his own knowledge on dress parade in the presence of one who could appreciate the display. But whenever any little thing released him for the time from conversation in the sitting room he was given to slipping out into the old kitchen, where, sitting on a chair that had no back, and leaning against the chimney side, he delighted to talk to Huldah. She couldn't talk much of books, but she could talk most charmingly of everything that related to the country life, and she could ask John many questions about the great city. In fact, John found that Huldah had come into possession of only such facts and truths as could be reached in her narrow life, but that she had assimilated them and thought about them, and that it was more refreshing to hear her original and piquant remarks about the topics she was acquainted with than to listen to the tireless stream of Janet Dunton's ostentatious erudition. And he found more delight in telling the earnest and hungry-minded country girl about the great world of men and the great world of books than in talking to Janet, who was, in the matter of knowledge, a little blasée, if I may be allowed the expression. And then, to Huldah he could talk of his mother, whom he had often watched moving about that same kitchen. When he had spoken to Janet of the associations of the old place with his mother's countenance, she had answered with a

88

quotation from some poet, given in a tone of empty sentimentality. He instinctively shrank from mentioning the subject to her again; but to Huldah it was so easy to talk of his mother's gentleness and sweetness. Huldah was not unlike her in these respects, and then she gave him the sort of sympathy that finds its utterance in a tender silence—so much more tender than any speech can be.

He observed often during the week that Huldah was depressed. He could not exactly account for it, until he noticed something in his sister's behavior toward her that awakened his suspicion. As soon as opportunity offered he inquired of Huldah, affecting at the same time to know something about it.

"I don't want to complain of your sister to you, Mr. Harlow—"

"Pshaw! call me John; and as for my sister, I know her faults better than you do. Go on, please."

"Well, it's only that she told me that Miss Dunton wasn't used to eating at the same table with servants; and when one of the boys told your father, he was mad, and came to me, and said, 'Huldah, you must eat when the rest do. If you stay away from the table on account of these city snobs I'll make a fuss on the spot.' So, to avoid a fuss, I have kept on going to the table."

John was greatly vexed with this. He was a chivalrous fellow, and he knew how such a remark must wound a person who had never learned that domestic service had anything degrading in it. And the result was just the opposite of what his sister had hoped. John paid more attention than ever to Huldah Manners because she was the victim of oppression.

The evening before Thanksgiving day the ladies were going to make a visit. It was not at all incumbent on John to go, but he was seeking an opportunity to carry off the brilliant Miss Dunton, who would adorn his parlors when he became rich and distinguished, and who would make so nice a headpiece for his table. And so he had determined to go with them, trusting to some fortunate chance for his opportunity.

But, sitting in the old "best room" in the dark, while the ladies were getting ready, and trying to devise a way by which he might get an opportunity to speak with Miss Dunton alone, it occurred to him that she was at that time in the sitting room waiting for his sister. To step out to where she was, and present the case in a few words, would not be difficult, and it might all be settled before his sister came downstairs. The Fates were against him, however; for, just as he was about to act on his thought, he heard Amanda Holmes's abundant skirts sweeping down the stairway. He could not help hearing the conversation that followed:

"You see, Janet, I got up this trip to-night to keep John from spending the evening in the kitchen. He hasn't a bit of dignity, and would spend the evening romping with the children and talking to Huldah if he took it into his head."

"Well," said Janet, "one can overlook everything in a man of your brother's culture. But what a queer way your country servants have of pushing themselves! Wouldn't I make them know their places!"

And all this was said with the kitchen door open, and with the intention of wounding Huldah.

John's castles tumbled. The erudite wife alongside the silver tea urn faded out of sight rapidly. If knowledge could not give a touch of humane regard for the feelings of a poor girl toiling dutifully and self-denyingly to support her family, of what account was it?

Two minutes before he was about to give his life to Janet Dunton. Now there was a gulf wider than the world between them. He slipped out of the best room by the outside door and came in through the kitchen. The neighbor's sleigh that was to call for them was already at the door, and John begged them to excuse him. He had set his heart on helping Huldah make mince pies, as he used to help his mother when a boy. His sister was in despair, but she did not say much. She told John that it was time he was getting over his queer freaks. And the sleigh drove off.

For an hour afterward John romped with his sister's children and told stories to the boys and talked to his father. When a man has barely escaped going over a precipice he does not like to think too much about it. John did not.

At last the little children went to bed. The old gentleman

90

grew sleepy, and retired. The boys went into the sitting room and went to sleep, one on the lounge and one on the floor. Huldah was just ready to begin her pies. She was deeply hurt, but John succeeded in making her more cheerful. He rolled up his sleeves and went to rolling out the pastry. He thought he had never seen a sweeter picture than the young girl in clean dress and apron, with her sleeves rolled above her elbows. There was a statuesque perfection in her well-rounded arms. The heat of the fire had flushed her face a little, and she was laughing merrily at John's awkward blunders in pie-making. John was delighted, he hardly knew why. In fixing a pie crust his fingers touched hers, and he started as if he had touched a galvanic battery. He looked at Huldah, and saw a half-pained expression on her flushed face.

For the first time it occurred to him that Huldah Manners had excited in him a feeling a thousand times deeper than anything he had felt toward Janet, who seemed to be now in another world. For the first time he realized that he had been more in love with Huldah than with Janet all the time. Why not marry her? And then he remembered what the governor had said about marrying a woman's heart and not her head.

He put on his hat and walked out—out, out, into the darkness, the drizzling rain, and the slush of melting snow, fighting a fierce battle. All his pride and all his cowardly vanity were on one side, all the irresistible torrent of his love on the other. He walked away into the dark wood pasture, trying to cool his brow, trying to think, and—would you believe it?—trying to pray, for it was a great struggle, and in any great struggle a true soul always finds something very like prayer in his heart.

The feeling of love may exist without attracting the attention of its possessor. It had never occurred to John that he could love or marry Huldah. Thus the passion had grown all the more powerful for not being observed, and now the unseen fire had at a flash appeared as an all-consuming one.

Turning back, he stood without the window, in the shadow, and looked through the glass at the trim young girl at work with her pies. In the modest, restful face he read the story of a heart that had carried great burdens patiently and nobly. What a glorious picture she was of warmth and light, framed in darkness! To his heart at that moment all the light and warmth of the world centered in Huldah. All the world besides was loneliness and darkness and drizzle and slush. His fear of his sister and of his friends seemed base and cowardly. And the more he looked at this vision of the night, this revelation of peace and love and light, the more he was determined to possess it. You will call him precipitate. But when all a man's nobility is on one side and all his meanness on the other, why hesitate? Besides, John Harlow had done more thinking in that half hour than most men do in a month.

The vision had vanished from the window, and he went in and sat down. She had by this time put in the last pie, and was sitting with her head on her hand. The candle flickered and went out, and there was only the weird and ruddy firelight. I can not tell you what words passed between John and the surprised Huldah, who had thought him already betrothed to Miss Dunton. I can not tell what was said in the light of that fire; I don't suppose Harlow could tell that story himself.

Huldah asked that he should not say anything about it till his sister was gone. Of course John saw that she asked it for his sake. But his own cowardice was glad of the shelter.

Next day a brother of John's, whom I forgot to mention before, came home from college. Mrs. Holmes's husband arrived unexpectedly. Aunt Judith, with her family, came over at dinner time, so that there was a large and merry party. Two hearts, at least, joined in the deacon's thanksgiving before dinner with much fervor.

At the table the dinner was much admired.

"Huldah," said Janet Dunton, "I like your pies. I wish I could hire you to go to Boston. Our cook never does so well."

John saw the well-aimed shaft hidden under this compliment, and all his manhood rallied. As soon as he could be sure of himself he said:

"You can not have Huldah; she is already engaged."

"How's that?" said Aunt Judith.

"Oh! I've secured her services," said John.

"What?" said Mrs. Holmes, "engaged your—your—your help before you engaged a wife!"

"Not at all," said John; "engaged my help and my wife in one. I hope that Huldah Manners will be Huldah Harlow by Christmas."

The deacon dropped his knife and fork, and dropped his lower jaw, and stared. "What! How! What did you say, John?"

"I say, father, that this good girl Huldah is to be my wife."

"John!" gasped the old man, getting to his feet and reaching his hand across the table, "you've got plenty of sense if you do wear a mustache! God bless you, my boy; there ain't no better woman here, nor in New York, nor anywhere, than Huldah. God bless you both! I was afraid you'd take a different road, though."

"Hurrah for our Huldah and our John!" said George Harlow, the college boy, and his brothers joined him. Even the little Holmes children hurrahed.

Here the judge stopped.

"Well," said Irene, "I don't think it was very nice in him to marry the 'help.' Do you, father?"

"Indeed I do," said the judge, with emphasis.

"Did she ever come to understand Emerson?" asked Anna, who detested the Concord philosopher because she could not understand him.

"Indeed I don't know," said the judge; "you can ask Huldah herself."

"Who? what? You don't mean that mother is Huldah?"

It was a cry in concert.

"Mother" was a little red in the face behind the copy of Whittier she was affecting to read.

1870

THE NEW CASHIER

My friend Macartney-Smith has working theories for everything. He illustrated one of these the other day by relating something that happened in the Giralda apartment house, where he lives in a suite overlooking Central Park. I do not remember whether he was expounding his notion that the apartment house has solved the question of co-operative housekeeping, or whether he was engaged in demonstrating certain propositions regarding the influence of the city on the country. Since I have forgotten what it was intended to prove, the incident has seemed more interesting. It is bad for a story to medicate it with a theory. However, here are the facts as Macartney-Smith relates them with his Q.E.D. omitted.

I do not know [he began] by what accident or on what recommendation the manager of the Giralda brought a girl from Iowa to act as clerk and cashier in the restaurant.

The new cashier had lived in a town where there were differences in social standing, but no recognized distinctions, after you had left out the sedimentary poverty-stricken class. She not only had no notions of the lines of social cleavage in a great apartment-house, but she had never heard of chaperonage, or those other indelicacies that go along with the high civilization of a metropolis. I have no doubt she was the best scholar in the arithmetic class in the village high school, and ten to one she was the champion at croquet. She took life with a zest unknown to us New Yorkers, and let the starchiest people in the house know that she was glad to see them when they returned after an absence by going across the dining-room to shake hands with them and to inquire whether they had had a good time. Even the gently frigid manner of Mrs. Drupe could not chill her friendliness; she was accustomed to accost that lady in the elevator, and demand, "How is Mr. Drupe?" whenever that gentleman chanced to be absent. It was not possible for her to imagine that Mrs. Drupe could be otherwise than grateful for any manifestation of a friendly interest in her husband.

To show any irritation was not Mrs. Drupe's way; that would have disturbed the stylish repose of her bearing even more than misplaced cordiality. She always returned the salutations of Miss Wakefield, but in a tone so neutral, cool, and cucumberish that she hoped the girl would feel rebuked and learn a little more diffidence, or at least learn that the Drupes did not care for her acquaintance. But the only result of such treatment was that Miss Wakefield would say to the clerk in the office: "Your Eastern people have such stiff ways that they make me homesick. But they don't mean any harm, I suppose."

Some of the families in the Giralda rather liked the new cashier; these were they who had children. The little children chatted and laughed with her across her desk when they came down as forerunners to give the order for the family dinner. If it were only lunch time, when few people were in the restaurant, they went behind the desk and embraced the cashier and had a romp with her. The smallest chaps she would take up in her arms while she pulled out the drawers to show them her paper knife and trinkets; and when there were flowers, she would often break off one apiece for even those least amiable little plagues that in an apartment house are the torment of their nurses and their mammas the livelong day. This not only gave pleasure to the infantry, but relieved an aching which the poor girl had for a once cheerful home, now broken up by the death of her parents and the scattering abroad of brothers and sisters.

The young men in the house thought her "a jolly girl," since she would chat with them over her desk as freely as she would have chatted across the counter with the clerks in Cedar Falls, where she came from. She was equally cordial with the head waiter, and with those of his staff who knew any more English than was indispensable to the taking of an order. But her frank familiarity with young gentlemen and friendly speech with servants were offensive to some of the ladies. They talked it over, and decided that Miss Wakefield was not a modest girl; that at least she did not know her place, and that the manager ought to dismiss her if he meant to maintain the tone of the house. The manager—poor fellow!—had to hold his own place against the rivalry of the treasurer, and when such complaints were made to him what could he do? He stood out a while for Miss Wakefield, whom he liked; but when the influential Mrs. Drupe wrote to him that the cashier at the desk in the restaurant was not a well-behaved girl, he knew that it was time to look out for another.

If the manager had forewarned her, she could have saved money enough to take her back to Iowa, where she might dare to be as friendly as she pleased with other respectable humans without fear of reproach. But he was not such a fool as to let go of one cashier till he had found another. It was while the manager was deciding which of three other young women to take that Mr. Drupe was stricken with apoplexy. He had finished eating his luncheon, which was served in the apartment, and had lighted a cigar, when he fell over. There were no children, and the Drupes kept no servant, but depended on the housekeeper to send them a maid when they required one, so that Mrs. Drupe found herself alone with her prostrate husband. The distracted wife did not know what to do. She took hold of the needle of the teleseme, but the words on the dial were confused; she quickly moved the needle round over the whole twenty-four points, but none of them suited the case. She stopped it at "porter," moved it to "bootblack," carried it around to "ice water," and successively to "coupe," "laundress," and "messenger-boy," and then gave up in despair, and jerked open the door that led to the hall. Miss Wakefield had just come up to the next apartment to inquire after a little girl ill from a cold, and was returning toward the elevator when Mrs. Drupe's wild face was suddenly thrust forth upon her.

"Won't you call a boy—somebody? My husband is dying," were the words that greeted Miss Wakefield at the moment of the apparition of the despairing face.

Miss Wakefield rushed past Mrs. Drupe into the apartment, and turned the teleseme to the word "manager," and then pressed the button three times in quick succession. She knew that a call for the manager would suggest fire, robbery, and sudden death, and that it would wake up the lethargic forces in the office. Then she turned to the form of the man lying prostrate on the floor, seized a pillow from the lounge, and motioned to Mrs. Drupe to raise his head while she laid it beneath.

"Who is your doctor?" she demanded.

"Dr. Morris; but it's a mile away," said the distracted woman. "Won't you send a boy in a coupé"

"I'll go myself, the boys are so slow," said the cashier. "Shall I send you a neighboring doctor till Dr. Morris can get here?"

"Do! do!" pleaded the wife, now wildly wringing her hands.

Miss Wakefield caught the elevator as it landed the manager on the floor, and she briefly told him what was the matter. Then she descended, and had the clerk order a coupé by telephone, and then herself sent Dr. Floyd from across the street, while she ran to the stable, leaped into the coupé before the horse was fairly hitched up, and drove for Dr. Morris.

Dr. Morris found Mrs. Drupe already a widow when he arrived with the cashier. The latter promptly secured the addresses of Mr. Drupe's brother and of his business partner, again entered the coupé, and soon had the poor woman in the hands of her friends.

The energetic girl went to her room that night exhilarated by her own prompt and kind-hearted action. But the evil spirit that loves to mar our happiness had probably arranged it that on that very evening she received a note from the manager notifying her that her services would not be required after one more week. On inquiry the next day she learned that some of the ladies had complained of her behavior, and she vainly tried to remember what she had done that was capable of misconstruction. She also vainly tried to imagine how she was to live, or by what means she was to contrive to get back to those who knew her too well to suspect her of any evil. She was so much perplexed by the desperate state of her own affairs that she even neglected to attend Mr. Drupe's funeral, but she hoped that Mrs. Drupe would not take it unkindly.

It was with a heavy heart that the manager called Miss Wakefield into his office on the ground floor in order that he might pay her last week's wages. He was relieved that she seemed to accept her dismissal with cheerfulness.

"What are you going to do?" he asked timidly.

"Why, didn't you know?" she said. "I am to live with Mrs. Drupe as a companion, and to look out for her affairs and collect her rents. I used to think she didn't like me. But it will be a good lesson to those ladies who found fault with me for nothing when they see how much Mrs. Drupe thinks of me."

And she went her way to her new home in Mrs. Drupe's apartment, at the end of the hall on the sixth floor, while the manager took from a pigeonhole Mrs. Drupe's letter of complaint against the former cashier, and read it over carefully.

The thickness of the walls at the base of so lofty a building made it difficult for daylight to work its way through the tunnel-like windows, so that in this office a gas jet was necessary in the daytime. After a moment's reflection the manager touched Mrs. Drupe's letter of complaint to the flame, and it was presently reduced to everlasting illegibility.

PRISCILLA

The trained novel readers, those who have made a business of it (if any such should honor this poor little story with their attention), will glance down the opening paragraphs for a description of the heroine's tresses. The opening sentences of Miss Braddon are enough to show how important a thing a head of hair is in the getting up of a heroine for the popular market. But as my heroine is not a got-up one, and as I can not possibly remember even the color of her hair or her eyes as I recall her now, I fear I shall disappoint the professionals, who never feel that they have a complete heroine till the "long waving tresses of raven darkness, reaching nearly to the ground, enveloping her as with a cloud," have been artistically stuck on by the author. But be it known that I take Priscilla from memory, and not from imagination. And the memory of Priscilla, the best girl in the school, the most gifted, the most modest, the most gentle and true, is a memory too sacred to be trifled with. I would not make one hair light or dark, I would not change the shading of the eyebrows. Priscilla is Priscilla forever, to all who knew her. And as I can not tell the precise color of her hair and eyes, I shall not invent a shade for them. I remember that she was on the blond side of the grand division line. But she was not blond. She was—Priscilla. I mean to say that since you never lived in that dear old-fogy Ohio River village of New Geneva, and since, consequently, you never knew our Priscilla, no words of mine can make you exactly understand her. Was she handsome? No—yes. She was "jimber-jawed"—that is, her lower teeth shut a little outside her upper. Her complexion was not faultless. Her face would not bear criticism. And yet there is not one of her old schoolmates that will not vow that she was beautiful. And indeed she was. For she was Priscilla. And I never can make you understand it.

As Priscilla was always willing to oblige any one, it was only natural that Mrs. Leston should send for her to help entertain the marquis. It was a curious chance that threw the young Marquis d'Entremont for a whole summer into the society of our little village. His uncle, who was his guardian, a pious abbé, wishing to remove him from Paris to get him out of socialistic influences, had sent him to New Orleans, consigned to the care of the great banking house of Challeau, Lafort & Company. Not liking to take the chances of yellow fever in the summer, he had resolved to journey to the North, and as Challeau, Lafort & Company had a correspondent in Henry Leston, the young lawyer, and as French was abundantly spoken in our Swiss village of New Geneva, what more natural than that they should dispatch the marquis to our pleasant town of vineyards, giving him a letter of introduction to their attorney, who fortunately spoke some book French. He had presented the letter, had been invited to dinner, and Priscilla Haines, who had learned French in childhood, though she was not Swiss, was sent for to help entertain the guest.

I can not but fancy that D'Entremont was surprised at meeting just such a girl as Priscilla in a rustic village. She was not abashed at finding herself face to face with a nobleman, nor did she seem at all anxious to attract his notice. The vanity of the marquis must have been a little hurt at finding a lady that did not court his attention. But wounded vanity soon gave place to another surprise. Even Mrs. Leston, who understood not one word of the conversation between her husband, the marquis, and Priscilla, was watching for this second surprise, and did not fail to read it in D'Entremont's eyes. Here was a young woman who had read. She could admire Corinne, which was much in vogue in those days among English-speaking students of French; she could oppose Saint Simon. The Marquis d'Entremont had resigned himself to the ennui of talking to Swiss farmers about their vineyards, of listening to Swiss grandmothers telling stories of their childhood in Neufchatel and Vaud. But to find in this young village school-teacher one who could speak, and listen while he spoke, of his favorite writers, was to him very strange. Not that Priscilla had read many French books, for there were not many within her reach. But she had read Grimm's Correspondence, and he who reads this has heard the echo of many of the great voices in French literature. And while David Haines had lived his daughter had wanted nothing he could get to help her to the highest culture.

100

But I think what amazed the marquis most was that Priscilla showed no consciousness of the unusual character of her attainments. She spoke easily and naturally of what she knew, as if it were a matter of course that the teacher of a primary school should have read Corneille, and should be able to combat Saint Simonism. As the dinner drew to a close, Leston lifted his chair round to where his wife sat and interpreted the bright talk at the other side of the table.

I suspect that Saint Simon had lost some of his hold upon the marquis since his arrival in a country where life was more simple and the manner of thought more practical. But he dated the decline of his socialistic opinions from his discussion with Priscilla Haines.

The next Sunday morning he strolled out of the Le Vert House, breathing the sweet air perfumed with the blossoms of a thousand apple trees. For what yard is there in New Geneva that has not apple trees and grapevines? And every family in the village keeps a cow, and every cow wears a bell, and every bell is on a different key; so that the three things that penetrated the senses of the marquis on this Sunday morning were the high hills that stood sentinels on every hand about the valley in which New Geneva stood, the smell of the superabundant apple blossoms, and the tinkle and tankle and tonkle of hundreds of bells on the cows grazing on the "commons," as the open lots were called. On this almost painfully quiet morning D'Entremont noticed the people going one way and another to the early Sunday schools in the three churches. Just as he came to the pump that stood in front of the "public square" he met Priscilla. At her heels were ten ragged little ruffians, whom she was accustomed to have come to her house every Sunday morning and walk with her to Sunday school.

"You are then a Sister of Charity also," he said in French, bowing low with sincere admiration as he passed her. And then to himself the young marquis reflected: "We Saint Simonists theorize and build castles in Spain for poor people, but we do not take hold of them." He walked clear round the square, and then followed the steps of Priscilla into the little brick Methodist church which in that day had neither steeple nor bell nor anything churchlike about it

101

except the two arched front windows. There was not even a fence to inclose it, nor an evergreen nor an ivy about it; only a few straggling black locusts. For the puritanism of New England was never so hard a puritanism as the Methodist puritanism of a generation ago in the West—a puritanism that forbade jewelry, that stripped the artificial flowers out of the bonnets of country girls, that expelled, and even yet expels, a country boy for looking with wonder at a man hanging head downward from a trapeze in a circus tent. No other church, not even the Quaker, ever laid its hand more entirely upon the whole life of its members. The dead hand of Wesley has been stronger than the living hand of any pope.

Upon the hard, open-backed, unpainted and unvarnished oak benches, which seemed devised to produce discomfort, sat the Sunday-school classes, and upon one of these, near the door, D'Entremont sat down. He looked at the bare walls, at the white pulpit, at the carpetless floors, at the general ugliness of things, the box stove, which stood in the only aisle, the tin chandeliers with their half-burned candles, the eight-by-ten lights of glass in the windows, and he was favorably impressed. With a quick conscience he had often felt the frivolous emptiness of a worldly life, and had turned toward the religion of his uncle the abbé only to turn away again antagonized by what seemed to him frivolity in the religions pomp that he saw. But here was a religion not only without the attractions of sensuous surrounding, but a religion that maintained its vitality despite a repelling plainness, not to say a repulsive ugliness, in its external forms. For could he doubt the force of a religious principle that had divested every woman in the little church of every ornament? Doubtless he felt the narrowness that could read the scriptural injunction so literally, but none could doubt the strength of a religious conviction that submitted to such self-denial. And then there was Priscilla, with all her gifts, sitting in the midst of her boys, gathered from that part of the village known as "Slabtown." Yes, there must be something genuine in this religious life, and its entire contrast to all that the marquis had known and grown weary of attracted him.

As eleven o'clock drew on, the little church filled with people.

102

The men sat on one side of the aisle and the women on the other. The old brethren and sisters, and generally those who prayed in prayer meeting and spoke in love feast, sat near the front, many of them on the cross seats near the pulpit, which were thence said by scoffers to be the "Amen corners." Any one other than a leader of the hosts of Israel would as soon have thought of taking a seat in the pulpit as on one of these chief seats in the synagogue. The marquis sat still and watched the audience gather, while one of the good brethren led the congregation in singing

"When I can read my title clear,"

which hymn was the usual voluntary at the opening of service. Then the old minister said, "Let us continue the worship of God by singing the hymn on page 554." He "lined" the hymn—that is, he read each couplet before it was sung. With the coming in of hymn books and other newfangled things the good old custom of "lining the hymn" has disappeared. But on that Sunday morning the Marquis d'Entremont thought he had never heard anything more delightful than these simple melodies sung thus lustily by earnest voices. The reading of each couplet by the minister before it was sung seemed to him a sort of recitative. He knew enough of English to find that the singing was hopeful and triumphant. Wearied with philosophy and blasé with the pomp of the world, he wished that he had been a villager in New Geneva, and that he might have had the faith to sing of the

"—land of pure delight
Where saints immortal reign,"

with as much earnestness as his friend Priscilla on the other side of the aisle. In the prayer that followed D'Entremont noticed that all the church members knelt, and that the hearty amens were not intoned, but were as spontaneous as the rest of the service. After reverently reading a chapter the old minister said: "Please sing without lining,

103

and then the old time of "Kentucky" was sung with animation, after which came the sermon, of which the marquis understood but few words, though he understood the pantomime by which the venerable minister represented the return of the prodigal and the welcome he received. When he saw the tears in the eyes of the hearers, and heard the half-repressed "Bless the Lord!" of an old brother or sister, and saw them glance joyfully at one another's faces as the sermon went on, he was strangely impressed with the genuineness of the feeling.

But the class meeting that followed, to which he remained, impressed him still more. The venerable Scotchman who led it had a face that beamed with sweetness and intelligence. It was fortunate that the marquis saw so good a specimen. In fact, Priscilla trembled lest Mr. Boreas, the stern, hard-featured "exhorter," should have been invited to lead. But as the sweet-faced old leader called upon one and another to speak, and as many spoke with streaming eyes, D'Entremont quivered with sympathy. He was not so blind that he could not see the sham and cant of some of the speeches, but in general there was much earnestness and truth. When Priscilla rose in her turn and spoke, with downcast eyes, he felt the beauty and simplicity of her religious life. And he rightly judged that from the soil of a cult so severe there must grow some noble and heroic lives. Last of all the class leader reached the marquis, whom he did not know.

"Will our strange brother tell us how it is with him to-day?" he asked.

Priscilla trembled. What awful thing might happen when a class leader invited a marquis, who could speak no English, and who was a disciple of Saint Simon, to tell his religious experience, was more than she could divine. If the world had come to an end in consequence of such a concatenation, I think she would hardly have been surprised. But nothing of the sort occurred. To her astonishment the marquis rose and said:

"Is it that any one can speak French?"

A brother who was a member of one of the old Swiss families volunteered his services as interpreter, and D'Entremont proceeded to tell them how much he had been interested in the exercises; that it was the first time he had ever been in such a meeting, and that he wished he had the simple faith which they showed.

Then the old leader said, "Let us engage in prayer for our strange brother."

And the marquis bowed his knees upon the hard floor.

He could not understand much that was said, but he knew that they were praying for him; that this white-haired class leader, and the old ladies in the corner, and Priscilla, were interceding with the Father of all for him. He felt more confidence in the efficacy of their prayers than he had ever had in all the intercessions of the saints of which he was told when a boy. For surely God would hear such as Priscilla!

It happened not long after this that D'Entremont was drawn even nearer to this simple Methodist life, which had already made such an impression on his imagination, by an incident which would make a chapter if this story were intended for the New York Weekly Dexter. Indeed, the story of his peril in a storm and freshet on Indian Creek, and of his deliverance by the courage of Henry Stevens, is so well suited to that periodical and others of its class, that I am almost sorry that Mrs. Eden, or Cobb, Jr., is not the author of this story. Either of them could make a chapter which would bear the title of "A Thrilling Incident." But with an unconquerable aversion to anything and everything "thrilling," the present writer can only say in plainest prose that this incident made the young marquis the grateful friend of his deliverer, Henry Stevens, who happened to be a zealous Methodist, and about his own age.

The effort of the two friends to hold intercourse was a curious spectacle. Not only did they speak different languages, but they lived in different worlds. Not only did D'Entremont speak a very limited English, while Stevens spoke no French, but D'Entremont's life and thought had nothing in common with the life of Stevens, except the one thing that made a friendship possible. They were both generous, manly men, and each felt a strong drawing to the other. So it came about that when they tired of the marquis's English and of the gulf between their ideas, they used to call on Priscilla at her home with her mother in the outskirts of the village. She was an interpreter indeed! For with the keenest sympathy she entered into the world in which the marquis lived, which had always been a sort of intellectual paradise to her. It was strange indeed to meet a living denizen of a world that seemed to her impossible except in books. And as for the sphere in which Stevens moved, it was her own. He and she had been schoolmates from childhood, had looked on the same green hills, known the same people, been molded of the same strong religious feeling. Nothing was more delightful to D'Entremont than to be able to talk to Stevens, unless it was to have so good an excuse for conversation with Priscilla; and nothing was so pleasant to Henry Stevens as to be able to understand the marquis, unless it was to talk with Priscilla; while to Priscilla those were golden moments, in which she passed like a quick-winged messenger between her own native world and the world that she knew only in books, between the soul of one friend and that of another. And thus grew up a triple friendship, a friendship afterward sorely tried. For how strange it is that what brings together at one time may be a wall of division at another.

I can not pretend to explain just how it came about. Doubtless Henry Stevens's influence had something to do with it, though I feel sure Priscilla's had more. Doubtless the marquis was naturally susceptible to religions influences. Certain it is that the socialistic opinions, never very deeply rooted, and at most but a reaction, disappeared, and there came a religious sentiment like that of his friends. He was drawn to the little class meeting, which seemed to him so simple a confessional that all his former notions of "liberty, fraternity, and equality" were satisfied by it. I believe he became a "probationer," but his creed was never quite settled enough for him to accept "full membership."

Some of the old folks could not refrain from expressions of triumph that "the Lord had got a hold of that French infidel": and old Sister Goodenough seized his hand, and, with many sighs and much upturning of the eyes, exhorted him: "Brother Markus, give up everything! give up everything, and come out from the world and be separated!" Which led D'Entremont to remark to Stevens, as they walked away, that "Madame Goodenough was vare curus indeed!" And Brother Boreas, the exhorter, who had the misfortune not to have a business reputation without blemish, but who made up for it by rigid scruples in regard to a melodeon in the church, and by a vicarious conscience which was kindly kept at everybody's service but his own—old Brother Boreas always remarked in regard to the marquis, that "as for his part he liked a deeper repentance and a sounder conversion." But the gray-haired old Scotch class leader, whose piety was at a premium everywhere, would take D'Entremont's hand and talk of indifferent subjects while he beamed on him his affection and Christian fellowship.

To the marquis Priscilla was a perpetual marvel. More brilliant women he had known in Paris, more devout women he had seen there, but a woman so gifted and so devout, and, above all, a woman so true, so modest, and of such perfect delicacy of feeling he had never known. And how poorly these words describe her! For she was Priscilla; and all who knew her will understand how much more that means than any adjectives of mine. Certainly Henry Stevens did, for he had known her always, and would have loved her always had he dared. It was only now, as she interpreted him to the marquis and the marquis to him, idealizing and elevating the thoughts of both, that he surrendered himself to hope. And so, toward the close of the summer, affairs came to this awkward posture that these two sworn friends loved the same woman.

D'Entremont discovered this first. More a man of the world than Henry Stevens, he read the other's face and voice. He was perturbed. Had it occurred two years before, he might have settled the matter easily by a duel, for instance. And even now his passion got the better for a while of all his good feelings and Christian resolutions. When he got back to the Le Vert House with his unpleasant discovery he was burning like a furnace. In spite of a rain storm just beginning and a dark night, he strode out and walked he knew not whither. He found himself, he knew not how, on the bank of the Ohio. He untied a skiff and pushed out into the river. How to advance himself over his rival was his first thought. But this darkness and this beating rain and this fierce loneliness reminded him of that night when he had clung desperately to the abutment of the bridge that spanned Indian Creek, and when the courage and self-possession of Henry Stevens had rescued him. Could he be the rival of a man who had gone down into the flood that he might save the exhausted marquis?

Then he hated himself. Why had he not drowned that night? And with this feeling of self-disgust added to his general mental misery and the physical misery that the rain brought to him, there came the great temptation to write "Fin," in French fashion, by jumping into the water. But something in the influence of Priscilla and that class meeting caused him to take a better resolution, and he returned to the hotel.

The next day he sent for Henry Stevens to come to his room.

"Henry, I am going to leave to-night on the mail boat. I am going back to New Orleans, and thence to France. You love Priscilla. You are a noble man; you will make her happy. I have read your love in your face. Meet me at the river to-night. When you are ready to be married, let me know, that I may send some token of my love for both. Do not tell mademoiselle that I am going; but tell her good-by for me afterward. Now, I must pack."

Henry went out stupefied. What did it mean? And why was he half glad that D'Entremont was going? By degrees he got the better of his selfishness.

"Marquis d'Entremont," he said, breaking into his room, "you must not go away. You love Priscilla. You have everything—learning, money, travel. I have nothing."

"Nothing but a good heart, which I have not," said D'Entremont.

"I will never marry Priscilla," said Henry, "unless she deliberately chooses to have me in preference to you."

To this arrangement, so equitable, the marquis consented, and the matter was submitted to Priscilla by letter. Could she love either, and if either, which? She asked a week for deliberation.

108

It was not easy to decide. By all her habits of thought and feeling, by all her prejudices, by all her religious life, she was drawn toward the peaceful and perhaps prosperous life that opened before her as the wife of Henry Stevens, living in her native village, near to her mother, surrounded by her old friends, and with the best of men for a husband. But by all the clamor of her intellectual nature for something better than her narrow life, by all her joy in the conversation of D'Entremont, the only man her equal in culture she had ever known, she felt drawn to be the wife of the marquis. Yet if there were roses, there were thorns in such a path. The village girl knew that madame la marquise must lead a life very different from any she had known. She must bear with a husband whose mind was ever in a state of unrest and skepticism, and she must meet the great world.

In truth there were two Priscillas. There was the Priscilla that her neighbors knew, the Priscilla that went to church, the Priscilla that taught Primary School No. 3. There was the other Priscilla, that read Chaucer and Shakespeare, Molière and De Staël. With this Priscilla New Geneva had nothing to do. And it was the doubleness of her nature that caused her indecision.

Then her conscience came in. Because there might be worldly attractions on one side, she leaned to the other. To reject a poor suitor and accept a rich and titled one, had something of treason in it.

At the end of a week she sent for them both. Henry Stevens's flatboat had been ready to start for New Orleans for two days. And Challeau, Lafort & Company were expecting the marquis, who was in some sort a ward of theirs. Henry Stevens and the Marquis Antoine d'Entremont walked side by side, in an awkward silence, to the little vine-covered cottage. Of that interview I do not know enough to write fully. But I know that Priscilla said such words as these:

"This is an awful responsibility. I suppose a judge trembles when he must pass sentence of death. But I must make a decision that involves the happiness of both my friends and myself. I can not do it now. Will you wait until you both return in the spring? I have a reason that I can not explain for wishing this matter postponed. It will be decided for me, perhaps."

I do not know that she said just these words, and I know she did not say them all at once. But so they parted. And Miss Nancy More, who retailed ribbons and scandal, and whose only effort at mental improvement had been the plucking out of the hairs contiguous to her forehead, that she might look intellectual—Miss Nancy More from her lookout at the window descried the two friends walking away from Mrs. Haines's cottage, and remarked, as she had often remarked before, that it was "absolutely scandalious for a young woman who was a professor to have two beaux at once, and such good friends, too!"

Gifted girls like Priscilla usually have a background in some friend, intelligent, quiet, restful. Anna Poindexter, a dark, thoughtful girl, was sometimes spoken of as "Priscilla's double"; but she was rather Priscilla's opposite: her traits were complementary to those of her friend. The two were all but inseparable; and so, when Priscilla found herself the next evening on the bank of the river, she naturally found Anna with her. Slowly the flatboat of which Henry Stevens was owner and master drifted by, while the three or four men at each long oar strode back and forward on the deck as they urged the boat on. Henry was standing on the elevated bench made for the pilot, holding the long "steering oar" and guiding the craft. As his manly form in the western sunlight attracted their attention, both the girls were struck with admiration. Both waved their handkerchiefs, and Henry returned the adieu by swinging his hat. So intent was he on watching them that he forgot his duty, and one of the men was obliged to call out, "Swing her round, captain, or the mail boat'll sink us."

Hardly was the boat swung out of the way when the tall-chimneyed mail boat swept by.

"See the marquis!" cried Anna, and again adieux were waved. And the marquis stepped to the guard and called out to Henry, "I'll see you in New Orleans," and the swift steamer immediately bore him out of speaking distance. And Henry watched him disappear with a choking feeling that thus the nobleman was to outstrip him in life.

"See!" said Anna, "you are a lucky girl. You have your choice; you can go through life on the steamboat or on the flatboat. Of course you'll go by steam."

"There are explosions on steamboats sometimes," said Priscilla. Then turning, she noticed a singular expression on Anna's face. Her insight was quick, and she said, "Confess that you would choose the flat-float." And Anna turned away.

"Two strings to her bow, or two beaux to her string, I should say," and she did say it, for this was Miss More's comment on the fact which she had just learned, that Miss Haines had received letters from "the lower country," the handwriting of the directions of which indicated that she had advices from both her friends. But poor Miss More, with never a string to her bow and never a beau to her string, might be forgiven for shooting popguns that did no harm.

There was a time when Priscilla had letters from only one. Henry was very ill, and D'Entremont wrote bulletins of his condition to Priscilla and to his family. In one of these it was announced that he was beyond recovery, and Priscilla and Anna mingled their tears together. Then there came a letter saying that he was better. Then he was worse again. And then better.

In those days the mail was brought wholly by steamboats, and it took many days for intelligence to come. But the next letter that Priscilla had was from Henry Stevens himself. It was filled from first to last with praises of the marquis; that he had taken Henry out of his boarding place, and put him into his own large room in the St. Charles; that he had nursed him with more than a friend's tenderness, scarcely sleeping at all; that he had sold his cargo, relieved his mind of care, employed the most prominent physicians, and anticipated his every want—all this and more the letter told.

And the very next steamboat from the lower country, the great heavy Duke of Orleans, with a green half moon of lattice work in each paddle box, brought the convalescent Henry and his friend. Both were invited to supper at the house of Priscilla's mother on the evening after their arrival. Neither of them liked to face Priscilla's decision, whatever it might be, but they were more than ever resolved that it should not in any way disturb their friendship. So they walked together to the cottage.

Priscilla's mother was not well enough to come to the table, and she had to entertain both. It was hard for either of the guests to be cheerful, but Priscilla at least was not depressed by the approaching decision. Equally attentive to both, no one could have guessed in which direction her preference lay.

"We must enjoy this supper," she said. "We must celebrate Henry's recovery and the goodness of his nurse together. Let's put the future out of sight and be happy."

Her gayety proved infectious, and as she served her friends with her own hands they both abandoned themselves to the pleasure of the moment and talked of cheerful and amusing things.

Only when they rose to leave did she allow her face to become sober, and even then the twilight of her joyousness lingered in her smile as she spoke, facing them both:

"How I have enjoyed your coming! I wanted us to have this supper together before coming to the subject you spoke of before leaving. I shall have to say what will give you both pain." There was a moment's pause. Then she resumed:

"The matter has been decided for me. I can marry neither of you. My father and all my brothers and sisters have died of consumption. I am the only one left of five. In a few months—" She lowered her voice, which trembled a little as she glanced toward her mother's room—"my poor mother will be childless."

For the first time, in the imperfect light, they noticed the flushed cheeks, and for the first time they detected the quick breathing. When they walked away the two friends were nearer than ever by virtue of a common sorrow.

And as day after day they visited her in company, the public, and particularly that part of the public which peeped out of Miss Nancy More's windows, was not a little mystified. Miss More thought a girl who was drawing near to the solemn and awful realities of eternal bliss should let such worldly vanities as markusses alone!

A singular change came over Priscilla in one regard. As the prospect of life faded out, she was no longer in danger of being tempted by the title and wealth of the marquis. She could be sure that her heart was not bribed. And when this restraint of conscience abnormally sensitive was removed, it became every day more and more clear to her that she loved D'Entremont. Of all whom she had ever known, he only was a companion. And as he brought her choice passages from favorite writers every day, and as her mind grew with unwonted rapidity under the influence of that strange disease which shakes down the body while it ripens the soul, she felt more and more that she was growing out of sympathy with all that was narrow and provincial in her former life, and into sympathy with the great world, and with Antoine d'Entremont, who was the representative of the world to her.

This rapidly growing gulf between his own intellectual life and that of Priscilla Henry Stevens felt keenly. But there is one great compensation for a soul like Henry's. Men and women of greater gifts might outstrip him in intellectual growth. He could not add one cell to his brain, or make the slightest change in his temperament. But neither the marquis nor Priscilla could excel him in that generosity which does not always go with genius, and which is not denied to the man of the plainest gifts. He wrote to the marquis:

"My dear Friend: You are a good and generous friend. I have read in her voice and her eyes what the decision of Priscilla must have been. If I had not been blind, I ought to have seen it before in the difference between us. Now I know that it will be a comfort to you to have that noble woman die your wife. I doubt not it will be a comfort to her. Do you think it will be any consolation to me to have been an obstacle in the way? I hope you do not think so meanly of me, and that you and Priscilla will give me the only consolation I can have in our common sorrow—the feeling that I have been able to make her last

113

days more comfortable and your sorrow more bearable. If you refuse, I shall always reproach myself.

"Henry."

I need not tell of the discussions that ensued. But it was concluded that it was best for all three that Priscilla and the marquis should be married, much to the disgust of Miss Nancy More, who thought that "she'd better be sayin' her prayers. What good would it do to be a march-oness and all that when she was in her coffin?"

A wedding in prospect of death is more affecting than a funeral. Only Henry Stevens and Anna Poindexter were to be present. Priscilla's mother had completed the arrangements, blinded by tears. I think she could have dressed Priscilla for her coffin with less suffering. The white dress looked so like a shroud, under those sunken cheeks as white as the dress! Once or twice Priscilla had drawn her mother's head to her bosom and wept.

"Poor mother!" she would say; "so soon to be alone! But Antoine will be your son."

Just as the dressing of the pale bride was completed, there came one of those sudden breakdowns to which a consumptive is liable. The doctor gave hope of but a few hours of life. When the marquis came he was heartbroken to see her lying there, so still, so white—dying. She took his hand. She beckoned to Anna and Henry Stevens to stand by her, and then, with tear-blinded eyes, the old minister married them for eternity!

Outside the door Priscilla's class of Slabtown boys stood with some roses and hollyhocks they had thought to bring for her wedding or her funeral, they hardly knew which. They were all abashed at the idea of entering the house.

"You go in, Bill," said one.

"No, you go. I can't do it," said Bill, scratching the gravel walk with his toes.

"I say somebody's got to go," said the first speaker.

"I'll go," said Boone Jones, the toughest of the party. "I ain't afeerd," he added huskily, as he took the flowers in his hand and knocked at the door.

But when Boone got in, and saw Priscilla lying there so white, he began to choke with a strange emotion. Priscilla tried to take the flowers from his hand, but Anna Poindexter took them. Priscilla tried to thank him, but she could only whisper his name.

"Boone — —" she said, and ceased from weakness.

But the lad did not wait. He burst into weeping, and bolted out the door.

"I say, boys," he repeated, choking his sobs, "she's just dyin', and she said Boone — you know — and couldn't say no more, and I couldn't stand it."

Feeling life ebbing, Priscilla took the hand of the marquis. Then, holding to the hand of D'Entremont, she beckoned Henry to come near. As he bent over her she whispered, looking significantly at the marquis, "Henry, God bless you, my noble-hearted friend!" And as Henry turned away, the marquis put his arm about him, but said nothing.

Priscilla's nature abhorred anything dramatic in dying, or rather she did not think of effect at all; so she made no fine speeches. But when she had ceased to breathe, the old preacher said, "The bridegroom has come."

She left an envelope for Henry. What it had in it no one but Henry ever knew. I have heard him say that it was one word, which became the key to all the happiness of his after life. Judging from the happiness he has in his home with Anna, his wife, it would not be hard to tell what the word was. The last time I was at his house I noticed that their eldest child was named Priscilla, and that the boy who came next was Antoine. Henry told me that Priscilla left a sort of "will" for the marquis, in which she asked him to do the Christian work that she would have liked to do. Nothing could have been wiser if she had sought only his own happiness, for in activity for others is the safety of a restless mind. He had made himself the special protector of the ten little Slabtown urchins.

Henry told me in how many ways, through Challeau, Lafort & Company, the marquis had contrived to contribute to his prosperity without offending his delicacy. He found himself possessed of practically unlimited credit through the guarantee which the great New Orleans banking house was always ready to give.

"What is that fine building?" I said, pointing to a picture on the wall.

"Oh! that is the 'Hospice de Sainte Priscille,' which Antoine has erected in Paris. People there call it 'La Marquise.'"

"By the way," said Priscilla's mother, who sat by, "Antoine is coming to see us next month, and is to look after his Slabtown friends when he comes. They used to call him at first 'Priscilla's Frenchman.'"

And to this day Miss More declares that markusses is a thing she can't no ways understand.

1871

TALKING FOR LIFE

For many years following the war I felt that I owed a grudge to the medical faculty. Having a romantic temperament and a taste for heroics, I had wished to fight and eat hard tack for my country. But whenever I presented the feeble frame in which I then dwelt, the medical man stood in my path with the remonstrance, "Why should you fill another cot in a hospital and another strip in the graveyard?" In these late years I have been cured of my regrets; not by service-pension slogans and pension agents' circulars, as you may imagine, but by the war reminiscence which has flooded the magazines, invaded every social circle, and rendered the listener's life a burden. In any group of men of my own age, North or South, I do not dare introduce any military topic, not even the Soudan campaign of General Wolseley, or the East Indian yarns of Private Mulvaney, lest I should bring down upon my head stories of campaigning on the Shenandoah, the Red River, or the Rappahannock—stories that have gained like rolling snowballs during the rolling years. Not that the war reminiscence is inherently tedious, but it is frightfully overworked. A scientific friend of mine of great endurance has discovered, by a series of prolonged observations and experiments at the expense of his own health, that only one man in twenty-seven hundred and forty-six can tell a story well, and that only one in forty-three can narrate a personal experience bearably. If I had gone into the army the chances are forty-two to one that I should have bored my friends intolerably from that day to this, and twenty-seven hundred and forty-five to one against my stories having anything engaging in them. I thank Heaven for the medical man that made me stay at home.

But once in a while it has been my luck to meet among old soldiers the twenty-seven hundred and forty-sixth man who can tell a story well. Ben Tillye is one of them, and here is an anecdote I heard from him, which is rather interesting, and which may even be true:

"I had just been promoted to a first lieutenancy, and thought

117

that I saw a generalship in the dim distance. Why, with such prospects, I should have straggled right into the arms of three bushwhackers, I do not know.

"Falling into the hands of guerrillas was a serious business then. An order had been issued by the wiseacre in command of the Army of the Potomac that all guerrillas taken should be put to death. This did not deprive the bushwhackers of a single man, but they naturally retaliated by a counter-order that all prisoners of theirs should be shot. In this game of pop and pop again the guerrillas had decidedly the advantage, and I was one of the first to fall in their way. I had hardly surrendered before I regretted that I had not resisted capture. I might have killed one of them, or at least have forced them to shoot me on the spot, which would not have been so much worse than dying in cold blood the next morning, and which would have led to a pursuit and the breaking up of their camp. But here I was disarmed, and after an hour's march seated among them bushwhacking in an old cabin on a hillside.

"The leader of the party of three who had captured me seemed a kindly man—one that, if it were his duty to behead me, would prefer to give me chloroform before the amputation. For obvious reasons I made myself as agreeable as possible to him. I tried also to talk to the captain of the band after I reached the camp, but he repelled my friendly advances with something like surliness. I reasoned that he intended to execute me, and did not wish to have his feelings taxed with regrets. At any rate, after finding that he could get no information of value from me, he went on with his writing at a table made by propping up an old wooden shutter in the corner of the cabin. Meantime I reflected that the only way in which I could avoid my doom was by awakening a friendly sympathy in the minds of my captors. I fell to talking for life. I trotted out my funniest stories, and the eight men about me laughed heartily as I proceeded.

"The captain was visibly annoyed. My interlocutor in this conversation was his second in authority, the one who had captured me. He had no distinct mark of rank, but I fancied him to be a sergeant. At length the captain turned to him, and said, 'Jones, I can't write if you keep up this talking.'

"I knew that this was meant as a hint for me, but I knew also that my very last hope lay in my winning the hearts of the guerrilla officer and his men. So with slightly lowered voice I kept on talking to the men, who looked at me from under their ragged slouched hats with the most eager interest. At the end of one of my stories their amusement broke forth into hearty laughter. The captain stopped writing, and turned upon me with the remark, only half in jest, I thought:

"'I'll have to shoot you, lieutenant. You must be a valuable man in the Yankee camp.'

"I forced a laugh, but went on with my stories, explaining to the captain that I meant to enjoy my last hours at all hazards. The accent of those about me reminded me irresistibly of the year that I, though of Northern birth, had spent in a school in eastern Virginia.

"'You are a Virginian,' I said to Sergeant Jones.

"'Yes.'

"'What county?'

"'I'm from Powhatan.'

"'I went to school in the next county,' I said, 'at what was called Amelia Academy.'

"'Goatville?' demanded Jones.

"'Yes, I went to old Goat. That's what we all called him on account of his red goatee. We never dated a letter otherwise than "Goatville." And yet we loved and revered the principal. Did you go there?'

"'No,' said Jones, 'but I knew a good many who did.'

"Well, from this I broke into my stock of schoolboy stories of the jokes about the 'cat,' or roll pudding we had twice a week, of the rude tricks put upon greenhorns and their retorts in kind. The men enjoyed these yarns, and even the captain was amused, as I inferred, because I could no longer hear his pen scratching, for he sat behind me.

"'Did you ever swim in the Appomattox?' asked Jones.

"'Yes,' I replied; 'I came near losing my life there once. I had a roommate who was a good swimmer. I was also a pretty good swimmer, and we foolishly undertook for a small wager to see who

119

could swim the river the oftenest, only stopping to touch bottom with our toes at each side. We went over side by side five times. The sixth crossing I fell behind; it was all I could do, and at its close I crept out on the bank and lay down. My roommate, Tom Freeman, struck out for a seventh. He was nearly over when the boys by my side uttered a cry. Tom was giving out. He was in a sort of hysterical laughter from exhaustion, and, though able to keep above the water, he could not make any headway. I got to my feet and begged the boys to go to his help, but they all had their clothes on, and they had so much confidence in Freeman as a swimmer that they only said, "He'll get out."

"'But I could see no way in which he could get out. I had recovered a little by this time, and I seized a large piece of driftwood, plunged into the river again, and pushed this old limb of a tree across the stream ahead of me. Freeman was sinking out of sight when he got his hand on the bough. I was able to push him into water where he could get a footing, but I somehow lost my own hold on the wood and found myself sinking, utterly faint from a sort of collapse. There was a tree that had fallen into the stream a few yards below. I was just able to turn on my back and keep afloat until I could grasp the top branches of the tree. Then I crept out—I never knew how, for I was only half conscious. But I'll never forget the cry from the boys on the other side of the stream that reached my ears as I lay exhausted alongside of Freeman on the bank. "Hurrah for Tilley!" they shouted.'

"'No, they didn't.' It was the captain who contradicted me thus abruptly, and I looked up in surprise.

"'That's not what they called you in those days,' said the captain. 'They shouted, "Hurrah for Stumpey!" They never called you anything but "Stumpey."'

"'Who in thunder are you?' I said, getting to my feet.

"'Tom Freeman,' replied the captain, rising and grasping my hand.

"Well, I wasn't shot, as you can see for yourselves."

PERIWINKLE

"Bring me that slate, Henriettar!"

Miss Tucker added a superfluous r to some words, but then she made amends by dropping the final r where it was preceded by a broad vowel. If she said idear, she compounded for it by saying waw. She said lor for law, and dror for draw, but then she said cah for car. Some of our Americans are as free with the final r as the cockney is with his initial h.

Miss Tucker was the schoolmistress at the new schoolhouse in West Easton. I am not quite sure, either, that I have the name of the place right. I think it may have been East Weston. Weston or Easton, whichever it is, is a country township east of the Hudson River, whose chief article of export is chestnuts; consequently it is not set down in the gazetteer. After all, it doesn't matter. We'll call it East Weston, if you please.

The schoolhouse was near a brook—a murmuring brook, of course. Its pleasant murmur could not be shut out. The school trustees had built the windows high, so that the children might not be diverted from their lessons by any sight of occasional passers-by. As though children could study better in a prison! As though you could shut in a child's mind, traveling in its vagrant fancies like Prospero's Ariel round about the earth in twenty minutes! The dull sound of a horse's hoofs would come in now and then from the road, and the children, longing for some new sight, would spend the next half hour in mental debate whether it could have been a boy astride a bag of turnips, for instance, or the doctor in his gig, that had passed under the windows.

It was getting late in the afternoon. Miss Tucker had dominated her little flock faithfully all day, until even she grew tired of monotonous despotism. Perhaps the drowsy, distant sounds—the cawing of crows far away, the almost inaudible rattle of a mowing machine, and the unvarying gurgle of the brook near at hand—had softened Miss Tucker's temper. More likely it had made her sleepy, for she relaxed her watchfulness so much that Rob

121

Riley had time to look at the radiant face of Henrietta full two minutes without a rebuke. At last Miss Tucker actually yawned two or three times. Then she brought herself up with a guilty start. Full twenty minutes had passed in which she, Rebecca—or, as she pronounced it, Rebekker—Tucker, schoolmistress and intellectual drum-major, had scolded nobody and had scowled at nobody. She determined to make amends at once for this remissness. Her eye lighted on Henrietta. It was always safe to light on Henrietta. Miss Tucker might punish her at any time on general principles and not go far astray, especially when she sat, as now, bent over her slate.

Henrietta was a girl past sixteen, somewhat tallish, and a little awkward; her hair was light, her eyes blue, and her face not yet developed, but there were the crude elements of a possible beauty in her features. When her temper was aroused, and she gathered up the habitual slovenly expression of her face into a look of vigor and concentrated resolution, she was "splendid," in the vocabulary of her schoolmates. She was one of those country girls who want only the trimmings to make a fine lady. Rob Riley, for his part, did not miss the trimmings. Fine lady she was to him, and his admiration for her was the only thing that interfered with his diligence. For Rob had actually learned a good deal in spite of the educational influences of the school. In fact, he had long since passed out of the possibility of Miss Tucker's helping him. When he could not "do a sum" and referred it to her, she always told him that it would do him much more good to get it himself. Thus put upon his mettle, Rob was sure to come out of the struggle somehow with the "answer" in his teeth. Miss Tucker would have liked Rob if Rob had not loved Henrietta, who was Miss Tucker's deadliest foe.

"Bring me that slate this instant!" repeated the schoolmistress when Henrietta hesitated, "and don't you rub out the picture."

Henrietta's face took on a sullen look; she rose slowly, dropping the slate with a clatter on her desk, whence it slid with a bang to the floor, without any effort on her part to arrest it. Miss Tucker did not observe—she was nearsighted—that in its fall, and in Henrietta's picking it up, it was reversed, so that the side presented to the schoolmistress was not the side on which the girl

122

had last been at work. All Miss Tucker saw was that the side which faced her when she took the slate from Henrietta's hand contained a picture of a little child. It was a chubby little face, with a funny-serious expression. The execution was by no means correct, the foreshortening of the little bare legs was not well done, the hands were out of drawing, and the whole picture had the stillness that comes from inexperience. But Miss Tucker did not see that. All she saw was that it was to her eye a miraculously good picture.

"That's the way you get your arithmetic lesson! You haven't done a sum this morning. You spend your time drawing little brats like that."

"She isn't a brat."

"Who isn't a brat?"

"Periwinkle isn't. That's Periwinkle."

"Who's Periwinkle?"

"She's my niece. She's Jane's little girl. You sha'n't call her a brat, neither."

"Don't you talk to me that way, you impudent thing! That's the way you spend your time, drawing pictures."

Miss Tucker here held the slate up in front of her and stared at the picture of Periwinkle. Whereupon the scholars who were spectators of Miss Tucker's indignation smiled. Some of them grew red in the face and looked at their companions. Little Charity Jones rattled out a good, hearty, irrepressible giggle, which she succeeded in arresting only by stuffing her apron into her mouth.

"Charity Jones, what are you laughing at?"

But Charity only stuck her head down on the desk and went into another snicker.

"Come here!"

Charity was sober enough now. Miss Tucker got a little switch out of her desk and threatened little Charity with "a good sound whipping" if she didn't tell what she was laughing at.

"At the picture," whimpered the child.

"I don't see anything to laugh at," said the mistress, holding the slate up before her.

Whereupon the school again showed signs of a sensation.

"What are you laughing at?" and Miss Tucker instinctively felt of her back hair.

"It's on the other side of the slate," burst out Charity's brother, who was determined to deliver his sister out of the den of lions.

Miss Tucker turned the slate over, and there was Henrietta's masterpiece. It was a stunning caricature of the schoolmistress in the act of yawning. Of course, when that high and mighty authority had, in her indignation held up the slate so as to get a good view of the picture of Periwinkle, she was unconsciously exhibiting to the school the character study on the reverse of the slate. And now, as she looked with unutterable wrath and consternation at the dreadful drawing, the scholars were full of suppressed emotion— half of it terror, and the other half a served-her-right feeling.

"The school is dismissed. Henriettar Newton will stay," said the schoolmistress. The children arose, glad to escape, while Henrietta felt that her friends were all deserting her, and she was left alone with a wild beast.

"Chaw her all up," said one of the boys to another. "I wouldn't be in there with her for a good deal."

Rob Riley left the room the last of all, and he lingered under the window. But what could he do? After a while he hurried away to Henrietta's father, on the adjoining farm, and made a statement of the case to him.

"I sha'n't interfere," said the old man sternly. "That girl's give me trouble enough, I'm sure. Spends her time makin' fool pictures on a slate. I hope the schoolmistress'll cure her."

Rob did not know what to say to this. He went back across the field to the schoolhouse door and sat down and listened. He could hear an angry collocation. He thought best not to interfere unless the matter came to blows.

The old man Newton entered his house soon after Rob Riley left him, and repeated to his wife what Rob had said from his own standpoint. The little grandchild, Periwinkle, sat on the floor with that funny-serious air that belonged to her chubby face.

"I'll go down and see about that, I will," she said with an air of great importance.

124

"What?" said the old man, looking tenderly and fondly at Periwinkle.

"I'll see about that, I will," said the barefoot cherub, as she pulled on her sunbonnet and set out for the schoolhouse, pushing resolutely forward on her sturdy little legs.

"I vum!" said the old man, as he saw her disappear round the fence corner.

The quaint little thing had not yet been in the house a week. She was sent on to the grandparents after her mother's death, and, as the child of the daughter who had left them years ago never to return, she had found immediate entrance into the hearts of the old folks. The reprobate Henrietta, who wasted her time drawing pictures, and who was generally in a state of siege at home and at school, had found in little Periwinkle, as they called her, a fountain of affection. And now that Henrietta was in trouble, the little Illinois Periwinkle had gone off in her self-reliant fashion to see about it.

When she reached the schoolhouse she found Rob Riley, whom she had come to know as Henrietta's friend, standing listening.

"I've come down to see about that, I have," said Periwinkle, nodding her head toward the schoolhouse. Then she listened a while to the angry voice of Miss Tucker, and the surly, sobbing, and defiant replies of Henrietta, who was saying, "Stand back, or I'll hit you!"

"Open that door this minute, Wob Wiley! I'm a goin' to see about that."

Rob hesitated. The latch was clearly out of Periwinkle's reach. Rob had a faint hope that the little thing might divert the wrathful teacher from her prey. He raised the latch and set the door slightly ajar.

"Now push," he said to Periwinkle.

She pushed the door open a little way and entered the schoolroom without being seen by the angry mistress, who was facing the other way, having driven Henrietta into a corner. Here stood the defiant girl at bay, waving a ruler, which she had snatched from the irate teacher, and warning the latter to let her

125

alone. Periwinkle walked up to the teacher, pulled her dress, and said:

"I've come down to see about that, I have."

"Who are you?" said the frightened Miss Tucker, to whom it seemed that the little chub had dropped down out of the sky, or come to life off Henrietta's slate.

"I'm Periwinkle, and you mustn't touch my Henrietta. I've come down to see about it, I have."

Miss Tucker, in a sudden reaction, sank down on a chair exhausted and bewildered. Then she sobbed a little in despair.

"What shall I do with that girl?" she muttered. "I'm beat out."

"Come home, Henrietta," said Periwinkle, and she marched Henrietta out the door under the very eyes of the schoolmistress.

"Come back this minute!" cried Miss Tucker, rallying when it was too late. But the weeping Henrietta, the solemn Periwinkle, and the rejoicing Rob Riley went away and answered the poor woman never a word.

Miss Tucker, who was not without some good sense and good intentions, found out that evening that she did not like teaching. She forthwith resigned the school in East Weston. In a week or two a new teacher was engaged, "a young thing from town," as the people put it, "who never could manage that Henrietta Newton."

But sometimes even a "young thing" is gifted with that undefined something that we call tact. Sarah Reade soon found out, from the gratuitous advice lavished upon her, that her chief trouble would be from Henrietta; so she took pains to get acquainted with the unruly girl the first day. Finding that the center of Henrietta's heart was Periwinkle, she took great interest in getting the girl to tell her all about Periwinkle. Henrietta was so much softened by this treatment that for three whole days after the advent of Miss Reade she did not draw a picture on the slate. But the self-denial was too great. On the fourth day, while Miss Reade was hearing recitation, and the girls at the desk behind Henrietta were looking over at her, she drew a cow very elaborately.

She was just trying to make the horns look right, rubbing them out and retouching them, while the other girls rose up in their seats and brought their heads together in a cluster to see, declaring in a whisper that "it was the wonderfullest thing how Henrietta could draw," when who should look down among them but Miss Reade herself. As soon as Henrietta became conscious of Miss Reade's attention she dropped her pencil, not with the old defiant feeling, but with a melancholy sense of having lost standing with one whose good opinion she would fain have retained.

The teacher took the slate in her hand, not in Miss Tucker's energetic fashion, but with a polite "Excuse me," which made Henrietta's heart sink down within her. For half a minute Miss Reade scrutinized the drawing without saying a word.

"Did anybody ever give you any drawing lessons?" she said to the detected criminal.

"No, ma'am."

"You draw well; you ought to have a chance. You'll make an artist some day. Your cow is not quite right. If you'll bring the picture to me after school I'll show you some things about it. I think you'd better put it away now till you get your geography lesson."

Henrietta, full of wonder at finding her art no longer regarded as a sin, put the slate into the desk, and cheerfully resumed the study of the boundaries and chief products of North Carolina, while Miss Reade returned to the hearing of the third-reader class.

"I say, Henrietta, she's j-u-s-t s-p-l-e-n-d-i-d!" whispered Maria Thomas. And Rob Riley thought Miss Reade was almost as fine as Henrietta herself.

"You see," said Miss Reade to Henrietta after school, "that the hind legs of your cow look longer than the fore legs."

"There's something wrong." said the girl, "but that isn't it. I've measured, and the cow's just as high before as behind, though she doesn't look so."

"Yes, but you've put her head a little toward you. The hind legs ought to seem shorter at a little distance off. Now try it. Make her not so high from the ground behind," and Miss Reade proceeded to explain one or two principles of perspective. When Henrietta had experimented on her cow and saw the result, she was delighted.

127

"I don't know much about drawing," said Miss Reade, "but I've a set of drawing books and some drawing cards. Now, if you'll let drawing alone till you get your lessons each day, I'll lend you my drawing books and give you all the help I can."

When the old man Newton heard that the "new school ma'am" was permitting Henrietta to draw "fool picters on her slate," he was sure that it never would work. He believed in breaking a child's will, for his part, "though the one that broke Henriettar's will would hev to git up purty airly in the mornin' now, certain," he added with a grim smile. But when the old man found Henrietta unexpectedly industrious, toiling over her studies at night, he was surprised beyond measure; and when he understood the compact by which studies were to come first and drawing afterward, he winked his eye knowingly at his wife.

"Who'd a thought that little red-headed school ma'am would a ben so cute? She knows the very bait for Henriettar now. That woman would do to trade hosses."

But when the little schoolmistress seriously proposed that he should send Henrietta down to New York to take lessons in drawing, he quickly changed his mind. Of what kind of use was drawing? And then, it would cost, according to Miss Reade's own account, about two or three hundred dollars a year for board; all to learn a lot of nonsense. It is true, when the teacher craftily told him stories of the prices that some lucky artists received for their work, he felt as though she were pointing down into a gold mine. But the money in his hand was good money, and he never sent good money after bad. And so Henrietta's newly raised hope of being an artist was dashed, and Rob Riley was grievously disappointed; for he was sure that Henrietta would astonish the metropolis if once she could take her transcendent ability out of East Weston into New York. Besides, Rob Riley himself was going off to New York to develop his own talent by learning the granite cutter's trade. He confided to Henrietta that he expected to come to something better than granite cutting, for he had heard that there had been granite cutters who, being, like himself, good at figures, in time had come to be great contractors and builders and bosses. He was going to be something, and when he was settled at work in New York Henrietta had a letter from him telling that he was learning mechanical drawing in the Cooper Union night school, and that he got books out of the Apprentices' Library. He also attended free lectures, and was looking out for a chance to be something some day. Henrietta carried the letter about with her, and wished heartily that she also might go to New York, where she could improve herself and see Rob Riley occasionally.

Now it happened that Mrs. Newton had a cousin, a rich man, in New York—at least, he seemed rich to those not used to the measure applied to wealth in a great city. She had not seen him since he left the little town in western Massachusetts, where they were both brought up. But she often talked about Cousin John. Whenever she saw his business advertisements in the papers she started out afresh in her talk about Cousin John. It is something quite worth the having—a cousin in New York whose name is in the papers, and who is rich. Whenever Mrs. Jones, Mrs. Newton's neighbor, talked too ostentatiously about her uncle, who was both a deacon and a justice of the peace up in New Hampshire, then Mrs. Newton said something about Cousin John. To save her life she couldn't imagine how Cousin John lived, except that he kept a carriage or two, or in what precisely his greatness consisted, since he held no office either in church or State, but the old lady evidently believed in her heart that a cousin who was a big man down in New York was nearly as good as an uncle who was a deacon up in New Hampshire.

Now it happened that John Willard, the Cousin John of Mrs. Newton's gossip, was spending the summer at Lebanon Springs, and at the close of his vacation he started to drive home through the beautiful region once the scene of the anti-renters' conflict with the old patroons. He stopped to see the Shaker villages, and then drove on among the rich farms, taking great pleasure in explaining to his town-bred wife the difference between wheat and rye as it stood in the shock, feeling for once the superiority of one whose early life has been passed in the country. He happened to remember that he had a cousin over in Weston, and though he had not seen her for many years, he proposed to turn aside and eat one dinner with old Farmer Newton and his wife.

And thus it happened that Cousin John Willard, and especially that Mrs. Cousin John Willard, saw Henrietta's drawings, and heard of her aspiration to learn to draw and paint; and thus it happened that Cousin John, and, what is of more consequence, Mrs. Cousin John, invited the girl to come down to New York and spend the winter with them and develop her talent for drawing; though Mrs. Willard did not think so much of Henrietta's developing her gift for art as that she had a fine face, and would undoubtedly develop into a beauty under city influences. And as Mrs. Willard had no children, and her house was lonesome, she thought it might add to her own consequence and to the cheerfulness of her house to have a handsome cousin under her care. Henrietta's father was rather unwilling to let her go; he didn't see how she could be spared from the housework; but the mother was resolved that she should go, and go she did.

The first things that excited the country girl's wonder were not the streets and buildings and the works of art, but the unwonted luxury of city life. Velvet carpets, large panes of plate glass, hot and cold water that came for the turning of a stopcock, illumination that burst forth as by magic, mirrors that showed the whole person and reduplicated the room—even doorbells and sliding doors, and dumb waiters and speaking-tubes, were things that filled her with astonishment. For weeks she felt that she had moved out of the world into a fairy book. But, being a high-spirited girl, she carefully concealed her wonder, moving about with apparent nonchalance, as though she had lived in the enchanted ground all her life. Secretly she carried on experiments upon water works, gas fixtures, and plate-glass mirrors, using the inductive method of reasoning, as all intelligent people have from the beginning, without any of the cumbrous and pedantic machinery provided for them by Lord Chancellor Bacon.

She was soon at work, but drawing from uninteresting plaster casts of scroll-work in the lower classes of the School of Design for Women was not so pleasant as spontaneous picture-making on her slate had been. In Weston, too, she had been a prodigy; her gift for drawing was little less than miraculous in the eyes of her companions. But in Cooper Institute she was one of many, and there were those whom much practice had rendered more skillful. She would slip away from her work and go through the alcoves sometimes, on one pretext or another, to envy the girls who were in their second year, and were drawing from a bust of Psyche or The Young Augustus, and especially did she wish that she were one of the favored circle in the Venus Room. She thought it would be fine to try the statue of the Venus de Milo. But day in and day out she had to stand before a cast of a meaningless scroll, endeavoring to represent it on drawing paper. This was no longer play, but work as tedious as the geography lessons in Weston. There is a great difference between work and play, though they both may consist in doing the same thing. Nevertheless Henrietta had positive ability, and the almost mechanical training of the first months did her good.

But somehow she was not so glad to see Rob Riley, the granite cutter, as she had expected to be. When Rob called at first to see her, the maid, who had received many warnings against allowing sneak thieves and tramps to stand in the hall, did not dare leave him by the hatrack. She eyed him suspiciously, cross-questioned him sharply, and finally called the cook upstairs to stand guard over him and the overcoats while she went to call Henrietta. Poor Rob, already frightened at having to ring the door-bell of a brown-stone house, stood in the hall fumbling his hat, while the stalwart cook never once took her eyes off him, but stood ready to throttle him if he made a motion to seize a coat or to open the door behind him. Somehow the greeting between the two under these circumstances was as different as possible from their parting in the country. Henrietta felt that by receiving Rob Riley in his Sunday clothes she had forever compromised herself with Hibernia downstairs; and poor Rob, half chilled by Henrietta's reception, and wholly dampened by the rosewood furniture and the lace curtains, and the necessity for sitting down on damask upholstery, was very ill at ease. Henrietta longed to speak freely, as she had done in the old days when they strolled through the hill pasture together, but then she trembled lest the door-bell should ring and some of Mrs. Cousin John's fine visitors enter the reception room. So the meeting was a failure. Rob even forgot that he had meant to ask Henrietta to go with him to the free lecture the next evening. And he was glad when he got out, and Henrietta was relieved, though she cried with vexation and disappointment when he was gone. As for Rob, he went home in great doubt whether it was worth while trying to be something. Of what use was it to seek to get to be a boss, a builder, or the owner of a quarry? Things were all wrong anyhow.

After this he only met Henrietta now and then as she came in or went out, though this was not easy, for he had to work with the hammer all day, and his evenings were spent in mechanical drawing. On second thought, he would be something, if only just to show folks that looked down on him. Though, if he had only known it, Henrietta did not look down on him at all; all her contempt was expended on herself.

But this feeling wore away as she became naturalized in Mrs. Cousin John's world. There were little dance parties, and though Henrietta was obliged to dress plainly, she grew more to be a beautiful woman. The simplicity of her dress set off this fine loveliness, and Henrietta Newton was artist enough to understand this, so that her clothes did not make her abashed in company. She had no party dresses, but with Mrs. Willard's assistance she always looked the beautiful country cousin. Other girls remarked upon the monotony of her dress, but then the gentlemen did not care that one woolen gown did duty on many occasions. Some women can stand the ordeal of a uniform for church and theater, party and tête-à-tête.

Mrs. Willard meant well by Henrietta. If Henrietta's art got on slowly, and her chance for a prize decreased steadily under the dissipating influences about her, it was not that Mrs. Willard intended to do her harm by parading her pretty cousin on Sundays and week days. It was only a second growth of vanity in Cousin John's wife. When one is no longer sought after for one's own sake, the next best thing is to be sought after for somebody else's sake. Mrs. Willard shone now in a reflected glory, as the keeper of the pretty Miss Newton. Young gentlemen stood squarely in front of Mrs. Willard and made full bows to her, and were delighted when she asked them to call. Mrs. Willard also carried it up to her own credit, in her confidential talks with ladies of her own age, that she was doing so much for John's cousin, whom she had found buried in an old farmhouse. For Mrs. Willard was a Christian and a philanthropist, besides being a reformer.

She was endeavoring with all her heart to reform a younger brother of her own, who was enough to have filled the hands of three or four red, white, and blue ribbon associations. He was a fine subject to work on, this young Harrison Lowder. Few young men have been so much reformed. He had a bright wit and genial manners, but moral endowments had been accidentally omitted in his makeup. Nothing that was pleasant could seem wrong to him. He was a magnificent sinner, with an artistic lightness of touch in wrongdoing, and he took his evil courses with such unfailing good nature that people forgave him.

It was a happy thought of Mrs. Willard's, when she saw him becoming fascinated with Henrietta, to reform him and render Henrietta a service at the same time. For Lowder had money, and to a poor country girl such a marriage ought to be a heaven-send, while it would serve to reform Harry, no doubt. It isn't always that a matchmaker can be sure of being a benefactor to both sides. One of the most remarkable things in nature, however, is the willingness of women to lay a girl's life on the altar for the chance of saving the morals of a scapegrace man. If a pious mother can only marry her son Beelzebub to some "good, religious girl," the chance of his reformation is greatly increased. The girl is neither here nor there when one considers the necessity for saving the dear Beelzebub.

Harry Lowder had the advantage of all other comers with Henrietta. The keeper was on his side, in the first place; and he was half domesticated at the house, coming and going when he pleased. The city dazzled the country girl, and it was a great pleasure to him to take her to theaters and operas. His winning manners, his apparent frankness, and the round of amusements he kept her in, could not but have their effect on a strong-willed creature such as

133

she was. Her pent-up intensity of life burst out now into the keenest enjoyment of all that she saw and heard and felt for the first time.

There were times when the memory of her country home and little Periwinkle came into her mind like a fresh breeze from the hills. At such times she recoiled from the round of unhealthful excitement in which she found herself; she hated the high-wrought plays and burlesque operas that she had seen; she despised the exciting novels that Harry Lowder had lent her. Then the old farm, with its stern and quiet ways, seemed a sort of paradise; she longed for her mother's voice, and even for her father's rebuke, for Rob Riley's homely love-making, and Periwinkle's quaint ways. At such times she had a sense of standing in some imminent peril, a dark foreboding shadowed her, and she wished that she had never come to New York, for the drawing did not get on well. Harry Lowder said it didn't matter about the drawing; she was meant for something better. There was always an easy way out of such depressions. Harry told her that she had the blues, and that if she would go to see this or that the blues would disappear. There is an easy way of getting rid of the blues by pawning to-morrow to pay to-day's debts.

It would hardly be right to say that Lowder was in love with Henrietta Newton, for in our good English tongue there is usually a moral element to the word love. But Harry certainly was fascinated with Henrietta—more fascinated than he had ever been with any one else. And as he had become convinced that it was best for him to marry and to reform—just a little—he thought that Henrietta Newton would be the girl to marry.

So it happened that Periwinkle, who had waited for Christmas to come that she might see Henrietta again, was bitterly disappointed. At Christmas Henrietta had been promised two great treats—Fox in Humpty Dumpty and the sight of St. Dives's Church in its decorations, with the best music in the city. And then there were to be other things quite as wonderful to the country girl. In truth, Henrietta was afraid to go home. Somewhere in the associations of home there lay in wait for her a revengeful conscience which she feared to meet. Then, too, Rob Riley would be at home, and a meeting with him must produce shame in her, and bring on a decision that she would rather postpone. Mrs. Willard begged her to stay, and it was hard to resist her benefactress. But in her girl's heart at times she was tired and homesick, and the staying in the city cost her two or three good crying spells. And when the holidays were past she bitterly repented that she had not gone home.

In this mood she sat down and wrote a long letter to her mother, full of regrets and homesickness, and longing and contradictoriness. She liked the city and she didn't. She hadn't done very well in her drawing, as she confessed, but she meant to do better. It was a letter that gave the good old mother much uneasiness. This city world was something that she could not understand—a great sea for the navigation of which she had no chart. She got from Henrietta's letter a vague sense of danger, a danger terrible because entirely incomprehensible to her.

And, indeed, she had already become uneasy, for when Rob Riley came home at Christmas time he did not come to see them, nor did he bring any messages from Henrietta. When she asked him about the girl, at meeting time on Sunday, Rob hung his head and looked at the toe of his boot a minute, and then said that he "hadn't laid eyes on her for six weeks." What did it all mean? Had Henrietta got into some disgrace? The father was alarmed also. He thought it about time that she should be getting a thousand dollars for a picture; though, for his part, he couldn't see why anybody should pay for a picture enough money to build two or three barns.

The little Periwinkle heard all of these discussions, though nobody thought of her understanding them.

"I'm going down there," she said. "I'm going to see about that, I am."

"What?" said the grandfather, looking at the little thing fondly.

"About Henrietta. I'm a-goin' down with Wob Wiley."

"Hello! you air, air you?"

Now it happened that in her fit of repentance and homesickness Henrietta had written: "I wish you would send dear little Periwinkle down here some time. I do want to see her, and she would be such a good model to draw from." Henrietta had not thought of the practical difficulties of getting the chubby little thing down, nor of how she would keep her if she came, nor, indeed, of the possibility of her words being understood in their literal sense. It was only a cry of longing.

But now the mother, full of apprehension and at her wits' end what to do, looked with a sort of superstitions respect at the self-confident little creature who proposed to go down to the city and see about things.

The old lady at first proposed to go down herself and take little Periwinkle with her; but she felt timid about the great city, and about Cousin John's fine ways of living. She wouldn't be able to find her way around, and she felt "scarr't" when she thought about it. Besides, who'd get father's breakfast for him if she went away?

So she decided to send Periwinkle down. Rob Riley could take her, and Cousin John's wife had always liked her and she'd be glad to see her. She hadn't any children of her own, and might be real glad to have the merry little thing about; and as for sending her back, there was always somebody coming up from the city. Of course Grandma Newton didn't think how large the village of New York had grown to be, and how unlikely it was that Henrietta should find any one going to Weston.

The greatest difficulty was to persuade Rob Riley to take her. His pride was wounded, and he didn't want to have anything to do with Henrietta and her fine folks. But the old lady persisted, and, above all, little Periwinkle informed Rob that she was going down to see about Henrietta. This touched Rob; he remembered when she had snatched Henrietta out of the jaws of Miss Tucker. He consented to take her to Mr. Willard's house and ring the door-bell.

Henrietta had recovered from her attack of penitence, and was again floating on the eddying current of excitement. One evening she went with Lowder to see La Dame aux Camelias. She had never before seen "an emotional play" of the French school, and it affected her deeply. Harry took advantage of her softened feelings to envelop her in a cloud of flattery, and to make love to her. Something of the better sense of the girl had heretofore held her back from any committal of her trust to him; but when they reached Mrs. Willard's parlor, Harry laid direct siege to Henrietta's affection, telling her what moral miracles her influence had wrought in him, and how nothing but her love was needed to keep him steadfast in the future; and, in truth, he more than half believed what he said. The whole scene was quite in the key of the play, and her overwrought feelings drifted toward the man pleading thus earnestly for affection. Harry saw the advantage of the situation, and urged on her an immediate decision. Henrietta, still shaken by passionate excitement, and without rest in herself, was on the point of promising eternal affection, in the manner of the heroine of the play, when there came a loud ringing of the door-bell. So highly strained were the girl's nerves, that she uttered a sharp cry at this unexpected midnight alarm. The servants had gone to bed when Henrietta came in. There was nothing for it but to open the door herself. With Harry Lowder behind her for a reserve, she timidly opened the front door, to find a child, muffled in an old-fashioned cloak and hood, standing upon the stoop, while a man was descending the steps. Looking around just enough to see who came to the door, he said, "Your mother said you wanted her, and she would have me bring her to you."

Then, without a word of good-night, Rob Riley walked away, Henrietta recognizing the voice with a pang.

"I come down to see about you," spoke the solemn and quizzical figure on the stoop.

"Where on earth did that droll creature come from?" broke out Lowder. "What is the matter, Miss Newton?"

For the suddenness of the apparition, the rude air with which Rob Riley had turned his back upon her, had started a new set of emotions in the mind of Henrietta. A wind from the old farm had blown suddenly over her and swept away the fog. She felt now, with that intuitive quickness that belongs to the artistic temperament, that she had recoiled but just in time from a brink. For a moment she seemed likely to faint, though she was not the kind of woman to faint when startled.

She reached out her hand to Periwinkle, and then, with a reaction of feeling, folded her in her arms and wept. Harry was puzzled. She suddenly became stiff and almost repellent toward him. She seemed impatient for him to be gone. It was a curious effect of surprise upon her nerves, he thought. He mentally confounded his luck, and said good night.

Henrietta bore Periwinkle off to her own room and removed her cloak, crying a little all the time. She was quite too full of emotion to take into account as yet all the perplexities in which she would be involved by the presence of Periwinkle in the house of Cousin John Willard.

"What brought you down here?" she said at last, when the sturdy little girl, divested of her shawl and cloak and mittens and hood, sat upon a chair in front of Henrietta, who sat upon the floor looking at her.

"I come down to see about you. Gran'ma said some things, and gran'pa said some things, and Wob Wiley he looked bad, and I thought maybe I'd just come down and see about you; and gran'ma said you wanted to make a picture of me. You don't want to make a picture to-night, do you? 'cause I'm awful sleepy. You see, Wob had to come on the seven o'clock twain, and that gits in at 'leven; and it took us till midnight to git here, and Wob he's got to go ever so fur yet. What made 'em build such a big town?" Here Periwinkle yawned and seemed about to fall off the chair. In a few minutes she was lying fast asleep on Henrietta's pillow.

But Henrietta slept not. It was a night of stormy trial. By turns one mood and then another dominated. At times she resolved to be a lady, admired and courted in the luxury of the city. As for possible consequences, she had never been in the habit of counting the cost of her actions carefully. There is a delicious excitement to a nature like hers in defying consequences.

But then a sight of Periwinkle's sleeping innocence sent back the tide with a rush. How much better were the simple old home ways and the love of this little heart, and the faithful devotion of that most kindly Rob Riley! She remembered her walks with him, her teasing him, his interference against Miss Tucker, and the deliverance wrought by the little creature lying there. She would go back to her old self, how painful soever it might be.

But she couldn't stay in the city and turn away Harrison Lowder; and to go home was to confess that she had failed in her art. And how could she humble herself to seem to wish to regain Rob Riley's love? And then, what kind of an outlook did the life of a granite-cutter's wife afford her? Here she looked at herself in the glass. All her pride rebelled against going home. But all her pride sank down when she stooped to kiss the cheek of the sleeping child.

In this alternation of feeling she passed the night. When breakfast time came she took Periwinkle down, making such explanations as she could with much embarrassment.

"You're sick, Henrietta," said Cousin John. "You don't eat anything. You've been working too steadily."

After breakfast the family doctor called, and said that Henrietta was suffering from too close application to her art, and from steam heat in the alcoves. She must have rest.

The poor, tired, perplexed girl, badgered with conflicting emotions, but resolved at last to escape from temptations that she could not resist effectually, received this verdict eagerly. She would go home; and the doctor agreed that change of scene was what she wanted. Her life in town was too dull.

Harry Lowder called that evening, but Henrietta had taken the precaution to be sick abed. At eight o'clock the next morning she was on the Harlem train.

"You see, I brought her home," said Periwinkle to her grandmother, in confidence. "I didn't like Cousin John's folks. They wasn't glad to see me; and I didn't like to leave Henrietta there."

But Henrietta, who had blossomed out into something quite different from the Henrietta of other times, made no explanation except that she was sick. For a week she took little interest in anything, ate but little, and went about in a dazed way, resuming her old cares as though she had never given them up. Somehow she seemed a fine lady in the dignity of manner and the self-possession that she had taken on with characteristic quickness of apprehension and imitation, and Mrs. Newton felt as if the housework were

139

unsuited to her. Even her father looked at her with a sort of respect, and forbore to chide her as had been his wont.

But when a week had passed she suddenly got out her material and began to draw. Periwinkle was set up first for a model, then her father and her mother, and then the dog, as he lay sleeping before the fire, had his portrait taken, to Periwinkle's delight. So persistent was her ambitious industry that every living thing on the place came in for a sketch. But Periwinkle was the favorite.

Rob Riley came home for July and August, the work in the yard being dull. He kept aloof from Henrietta, and she nodded to him with a severe and almost disdainful air that made him wretched. After three or four weeks of this coolness, during which Henrietta got a reputation for pride in the whole country, Rob grew desperate. What did he care for the "stuck-up" girl? He would have it out, anyhow, the next time he had a chance.

They met one day on the little bridge that crossed the brook near the schoolhouse. Henrietta nodded a bare recognition.

"You didn't treat me that way once, Henrietta. What's the matter? Have I done anything wrong? Can't you be friendly?"

"Why don't you be friendly?" said the girl, looking down.

"I—I?" said Rob.

"You haven't spoken to me since you came home."

"Well, that isn't my fault; you wouldn't look at me. I'm not going to run after a person that lives in a fine house and that only nods her head at me."

"I don't live in a fine house, but in that old frame."

"Well, why don't you be friendly?"

"It isn't a girl's place to be friendly first, is it?"

Rob stared at her.

"But you had other young men come to see you in town, and—you know I couldn't."

"I don't live in town now."

"What made you come home?"

"If I'd wanted to I might have stayed there and had 'other young men,' as you call them, coming to see me yet."

Rob gasped, but said nothing.

140

"Are you going over to Mr. Brown's?" asked Henrietta, to break the awkward silence that followed, at the same time moving toward home.

"Well—no," said Rob; "I think I'm going to your house, if you've no objection," and he laughed, a foolish little laugh.

"Periwinkle was asking about you this morning," said Henrietta evasively as they walked on toward Mr. Newton's.

Having once fallen into the old habit of going to Mr. Newton's, Rob could never get out of the way of walking down that lane. Just to see how Henrietta got on with her drawing, as he said, he went there every evening. He confided to Henrietta that he had shown such proficiency in "figures" in the night school that he was to have a place in a civil engineer's office when he returned to the city in the fall. It wasn't much of a place; the salary was small, but it gave him an opportunity to study and a chance of being something some day.

And Henrietta went on with her drawing, but without ever saying anything about a return to Cousin John's. And, indeed, she never did go back to Cousin John's from that day to this. She spent three years in Weston. If they were tedious years, she said nothing about them. Rob came home on Christmas and for a week in summer. Once in a long time he would run up the Harlem road on Saturday evening. These were white Sundays when Rob was at home, for then he and Henrietta went to meeting together, and sat on the porch in the afternoons while Rob told her how he expected to be somebody some day.

But being somebody is hard work and slow for most of us, as Rob Riley found out. His salary was not increased very fast, but he made up for that by steadily increasing his knowledge and his value in the office. For Rob had discovered that being somebody means being something. You can't hide any man under a bushel if he has a real light in him.

It was not till last year that Henrietta returned to the city. She is a student now in oil painting. But she does not live at Cousin John's. Nor, indeed, does she live in a very fashionable street, if I must confess it. There are many old houses in New York that have

141

been abandoned by their owners because of the uptown movement and the west-side movement of fashion. These houses are as quaint in their antique interiors as a bric-a-brac cabinet. In an upper story of one of these subdivided houses Rob Riley and his wife, Henrietta, have two old-fashioned rooms; the front room is large and airy, with a carved mantelpiece, the back room small and cosy. The furniture is rather plain and scant, for Rob has not yet got to be a great engineer working on his own account. At present he is one of those little fish that the big fish are made to eat—an obscure man whose brains are carried up to the credit of his chief. But he is already something, and is sure to be somebody. And, for that matter, the rooms in the old mansion in De Witt Place are quite good enough for two stout-hearted young people who are happy. The walls are well ornamented with pictures from Henrietta's own brush and pencil. These are not framed, but tacked up wherever the light is good. The best of them is a chubby little girl with a droll-serious air, clad in an old-fashioned hood and muffled in cloaks and shawls. It is a portrait of Periwinkle as she stood that night on Cousin John's steps when she had come down to see about Henrietta.

Henrietta is just finishing a picture called The Culprit, which she hopes will be successful. It represents a girl in a country school arraigned for drawing pictures on a slate. Rob, at least, thinks it very fine, but he is not a harsh critic of anything Henrietta makes.

Rob was talking one evening, as usual, about the time when he should come to be somebody. But Henrietta said: "O Rob, things are nice enough as they are; I don't believe we'd be any happier in a house as fine as Cousin John's. Let's have a good time as we go along, and not mind about being somebody. But, Rob, I wish somebody'd buy this picture, and then we could have something to set off this room a little. Don't you think a sofa would be nice?" And then she looked at him, and said, "You dear, good old Rob, you!" though why she should call him old, or what connection this remark had with the previous conversation, I do not know.

THE CHRISTMAS CLUB

A GHOST STORY

"The Dickens!"

That was just what Charley Vanderhuyn said that Christmas Eve, and as a faithful historian I give the exact words. It sounded like swearing, though why we should regard it profane to make free with the devil's name, or even his nickname, I never could see. Can you? Besides, there was some ambiguity about Charley's use of the word under the circumstances, and he himself couldn't tell whether his exclamation had reference to the Author of Evils or only to the Author of Novels. The circumstances were calculated to suggest equally thoughts of the Great Teller of Stories and of the Great Story-teller, and I have a mind to amuse you at this Christmas season by telling you the circumstances, and letting you decide, if you can, which Dickens it was that Charles Vanderhuyn intended.

Charley Vanderhuyn was one of those young men that could grow nowhere on this continent except in New York. He had none of the severe dignity that belongs to a young man of wealth who has passed his life in sight of long rows of red brick houses with clean doorsteps and white wooden shutters. Something of the venerableness of Independence Hall, the dignity of Girard College, and the air of financial importance that belongs to the Mint gets into the blood of a Philadelphian. Charley had none of that. Neither did he have that air of profound thought, that Adams-Hancock-Quincy-Webster-Emerson-Sumner look that is the inevitable mark of Beacon Street. When you see such a young man you know that he has grown part of Faneuil Hall, and the Common, and the Pond, and the historic elm. He has lived where the very trees are learned and carry their Latin names about with them. Charley had none of the "vim" and dash that belongs to a Westerner. He was of the metropolis—metropolitan. He had good blood in him, else he could never have founded the Christmas Club, for you can not get more out of a man than there is in his blood. Charley Vanderhuyn bore a good old Dutch name—I have heard that the Van der Huyns were a famous and noble family; his Dutch blood was mingled with other good strains, and the whole was mellowed into generousness and geniality in generations of prosperous ancestors; for the richest and choicest fruit (and the rankest weeds as well!) can be produced only in the sunlight. And a very choice fruit of a very choice stock was and is our Charley Vanderhuyn. That everybody knows who knows him now, and that we all felt who knew him earlier in the days of the Hasheesh Club.

You remember the Hasheesh Club, doubtless. In its day it numbered the choicest spirits in New York, and the very center of all of them was this same Charley Vanderhuyn, whose face, the boys used to say, was like the British Empire—for on it the sun never set. His unflagging spirits, his keen love for society, his quick sympathy with everybody, his fine appreciation of every man's good points, whatever they might be, made Charley a prince wherever he went. I said he was the center of the circle of young men about the Hasheesh Club ten years ago; and so he was, though, to tell the truth, he was then but about twenty-one years of age. They had a great time at the club, I remember, when he came of age and came into possession of his patrimony—a trifle of half a million, I believe. He gave a dinner, and there was such a time as the Hasheesh Club never saw before nor since. I fear there was overmuch wine-drinking, and I am sure there was a fearful amount of punch drunk. Charley never drank to excess, never lost his self-control for a moment under any temptation. But there was many another young man, of different temperament, to whom the rooms of the club were what candles are to moths. One poor fellow, who always burned his wings, was a blue-eyed, golden-haired young magazine writer of that day. We all thought of his ability and promise—his name was John Perdue, but you will doubtless remember him by his nom de plume of "Baron Bertram." Poor fellow! he loved Charley passionately, and always drank himself drunk at the club. He wasted all he had and all he made; his clothes grew shabby, he borrowed of Charley, who was always open-handed, until his pride would allow him to borrow no more. He had just married, too, and he was so ashamed of his own wreck that he completed his ruin by drinking to forget it.

I am not writing a story with a temperance moral; temperance tales are always stupid and always useless. The world is brimful of walking morals on that subject, and if one will not read the lesson of the life of his next-door neighbor, what use of bringing Lazarus from the dead to warn him of a perdition that glares at him out of the eyes of so many men?

I mentioned John Perdue—poor golden-haired "Baron Bertram"—only because he had something to do with the circumstances which led Charley Vanderhuyn to use that ambiguous interjection about "the Dickens!" Perdue, as I said, dropped away from the Hasheesh Club, lost his employment as literary editor of the Luminary, fell out of good society, and at last earned barely enough to keep him and his wife and his child in bread, and to supply himself with whisky, by writing sensation stories for the "penny dreadfuls." We all suspected that he would not have received half so much for his articles had they been paid for on their merits or at the standard price for hack writing. But Charley Vanderhuyn had something to do with it. He sent Henry Vail—he always sent Henry Vail on his missions of mercy—to find out where Perdue sold his articles, and I have no doubt the price of each article was doubled, at Vanderhuyn's expense.

And that mention of Henry Vail reminds me that I can not tell this story rightly unless I let you know who he was. A distant relation of Charley's, I believe. He was a studious fellow from the country, and quite awkward in company. The contrast between him and Charley was marked. Vanderhuyn was absolutely au fait in all the usages of society; he knew by instinct how a thing ought to be done, and his example was law. He had a genius for it, everybody said. Vail was afraid of his shadow; did not know just what was proper to do in any new circumstances. His manners hung about him loosely; Vanderhuyn's were part of himself. When Vail came to the Hasheesh Club for the first time it was on the occasion of Charley's majority dinner. Vail consulted Vanderhuyn about his costume, and was told that he must wear evening dress; and, never having seen anything but provincial society, he went with perfect assurance to a tailor's and ordered a new frock coat and a white vest. When he saw that the other gentlemen present wore dress coats, and that most of them had black vests, he was in some consternation. He even debated whether he should not go out and hire a dress coat for the evening. He drew Charley aside, and asked him why he did not tell him that those sparrow-tail things had come into fashion again!

But he never took kindly to the club life; he soon saw that however harmless it might be to some men, it was destruction to others. After attending a few times, Henry Vail, who was something of a Puritan and much of a philanthropist, declared his opposition to what he called an English dissipation.

Henry Vail was a scholarly fellow, of real genius, and had studied for the ministry; but he had original notions, and about the time he was to have taken deacon's orders in the Episcopal Church he drew back. He said that orders would do for some men, but he did not intend to build a wall between himself and his fellows. He could do more by remaining a man of like passions with other men than he could by casing himself in a clerical "strait-jacket," as he called it. Having a little income of his own, he set up on his own account in the dingiest part of that dingy street called Huckleberry Street—the name, with all its suggestions of fresh fields and pure air and liberty, is a dreary mockery. Just where Greenfield Court—the dirtiest of New York alleys—runs out of Huckleberry Street, he set up shop, to use his own expression, He was a kind of independent lay clergyman, ministering to the physical and spiritual wants of his neighbors, climbing to garrets and penetrating to cellars, now talking to a woman who owned a candy and gingerbread stall, and now helping to bury a drunken sailor. Such a life for a scholar! But he always declared that digging out Greek and Hebrew roots was not half so fascinating a work as digging out human souls from the filth of Huckleberry Street.

Of course he did not want for money to carry on his operations. Charley Vanderhuyn's investments brought large returns, and Charley knew how to give. When Vail would begin a pathetic story, Vanderhuyn would draw out his check book, and say: "How much shall it be, Harry?—never mind the story. It's handy to have you to give away my money for me. I should never take the trouble to see that it went to the people that need. One dollar given by you is worth ten that I bestow on Tom, Dick, and Harry; so I prefer to let Tom and Dick go without, and give it all to Harry." In fact Vanderhuyn had been the prey of so many impostors that he adopted the plan of sending all of his applicants to Vail, with a note to him, which generally ran thus, "Please investigate." The tramps soon ceased to trouble him, and then he took to intrusting to Vail each month a sum equal to what he had been in the habit of giving away loosely.

It was about the first of December, four years ago, that Harry Vail, grown younger and fresher in two years of toil among the poor—glorified he seemed by the tenderness of his sympathies and the nobleness of his aims—it was four years ago that Harry came into Charley Vanderhuyn's rooms for his regular monthly allotment. Vail generally came in the evening, and Charley generally managed to be disengaged for that evening. The two old friends whose paths diverged so widely were fond of each other's company, and Vail declared that he needed one evening in the month with Vanderhuyn; he liked to carry away some of Charley's sunshine to the darkness of Huckleberry Street and Greenfield Court. And Charley said that Harry brought more sunlight than he took. I believe he was right. Charley, like all men who live without a purpose, was growing less refined and charming than he had been, his cheeks were just a trifle graver than those of the young Charley had been. But he talked magnificently as ever. Vail said that he himself was an explorer in a barbarous desert, and that Charles Vanderhuyn was the one civilized man he could meet.

It is a curious thing that Vail had never urged Charley to a different life from the self-indulgent one that he led, but it was a peculiarity of Henry's that he was slow to attack a man directly. I have heard that it was one great secret of his success among the poor, that he would meet an intemperate man twenty times,

147

perhaps, before he attacked his vice. Then, when the man had ceased to stand guard, Vail would suddenly find an entrance to him by an unwatched gate. It was remarkable, too, that when he did seize on a man he never for an instant relaxed his grasp. I have often looked at his aquiline nose, and wondered if it were not an index to this eagle-like swoop at the right moment, and this unwavering firmness of hold.

On this evening, about the first of December, four years ago, he sat in Charley's cozy bedroom and listened to Vanderhuyn's stories of a life antipodal to the life he was accustomed to see—for the antipodes do not live round the world, but round the first street corner; he listened and laughed at the graphic and eloquent and grotesque pictures that Charley drew for him till nearly midnight, and then got ready to go back to his home, among the noisy saloons of Huckleberry Street. Charley drew out his check book and wrote and tore off the check, and handed it to Vail.

"I want more, Charley, this time," said Vail in his quiet, earnest way, with gray eyes fixed on his friend's blue ones.

"Got more widows without coal than usual, eh, old fellow? How much shall it be? Double? Ask anything. I can't refuse the half of my fortune to such a good angel as you are, Vail. I don't spend any money that pays so well as what I give you. I go to the clubs and to parties. I sit at the opera and listen to Signora Scracchioli, and say to myself, 'Well, there's Vail using my money to help some poor devil in trouble.' I tell you I get a comfortable conscience by an easy system of commutation. Here, exchange with me; this is for double the amount, and I am glad you mentioned it."

"But I want more than that this time," and Vail fixed his eyes on Charley in a way that made the latter feel just a little ill at ease, a sensation very new to him.

"Well, how much, Harry? Don't be afraid to ask. I told you you should have half my kingdom, old fellow!" And Vanderhuyn took his pen and began to date another check.

"But, Charley, I am almost afraid to ask. I want more than half you have—I want something worth more than all you have."

"Why, you make me curious. Never saw you in that vein

before, Vail," and Charley twisted a piece of paper, lighted it in the gas jet, and held it gracefully in his fingers while he set his cigar going, hoping to hide his restlessness under the wistful gaze of his friend by this occupation of his attention.

But however nervous Henry Vail might be in the performance of little acts that were mere matters of convention, there was no lack of quiet self-possession in matters that called out his earnestness of spirit. And now he sat gazing steadily at Charley until the cigar had been gracefully lighted, the bit of paper tossed on the grate, and until Charley had watched his cigar a moment. When the latter reluctantly brought his eyes back into range with the dead-earnest ones that had never ceased to look on him with that strange wistful expression, then Henry Vail proceeded:

"I want you, Charley."

Charley laughed heartily now. "Me? What a missionary I would make! Kid-glove gospeller I'd be called in the first three days. What a superb Sunday-school teacher I'd make! Why, Henry Vail, you know better. There's just one thing in this world I have a talent for, and that's society. I'm a man of the world in my very fiber. But as for following in your illustrious footsteps—I wish I could be so good a man, but you see I'm not built in that way. I'm a man of the world."

"That's just what I want," said Henry Vail, looking with the same tender wistfulness into his friend's eyes. "If I'd wanted a missionary I shouldn't have come to you. If I'd wanted a Sunday-school teacher I could have found twenty better; and as for tract distributing and Bible reading, you couldn't do either if you'd try. What I want for Huckleberry Street more than I want anything else is a man of the world. You are a man of the world—of the whole world. I have seen a restaurant waiter stop and gape and listen to your talk. I have seen a coal-heaver delighted with your manners when you paid him. Charley, you're the most magnificent man of the world I ever saw. Must a man of the world be useless? I tell you I want you for God and Huckleberry Street, and I mean to have you some day, old fellow." And the perfect assurance with which he said this, and the settled conviction of final success that was visible in his quiet gray eyes, fascinated Charley Vanderhuyn, and he felt spellbound, like the wedding guest held by the "Ancient Mariner."

"I tell you what, Henry," he said presently, "I've got no call. I'm an Epicurean. I say to you, in the words of an American poet:

> 'Take the current of your nature, make it stagnant if you will:
> Dam it up to drudge forever at the service of your will.
> Mine the rapture and the freedom of the torrent on the hill!
> I shall wander o'er the meadows where the fairest blossoms call:
> Though the ledges seize and fling me headlong from the rocky wall,
> I shall leave a rainbow hanging o'er the ruins of my fall.'"

"Charley, I don't want to preach," said Vail; "but you know that this doctrine of mere selfish floating on the current of impulse which your traveler poet teaches is devilish laziness, and devilish laziness always tends to something worse. You may live such a life, and quote such poetry, but you don't believe that a man should flow on like a purposeless river. The lines you quoted bear the mark of a restless desire to apologize to conscience for a fearful waste of power and possibility. No," he said, rising, "I don't want that check. This one will do; but you won't forget that God and Huckleberry Street want you, and they will have you, too, noble-hearted fellow! Good night! God bless you!" and he shook Charley's hand and went out into the night to seek his home in Huckleberry Street. And the genial Charley never saw his brave friend again. Yes, he did, too. Or did he?

II

The month of December, four years ago, was a month of much festivity in the metropolis. Charley was wanted nearly every night to grace some gathering or other, and Charley was too obliging to refuse to go where he was wanted—that is, when he was wanted in Fifth Avenue or Thirty-fourth Street.[3] As for Huckleberry Street and Greenfield Court, they were fast fading out of Charley's mind. He knew that Henry Vail would introduce the subject when he came for his January check, and he expected some annoyance from the discussion of the question—annoyance, because there was something in his own breast that answered to Vail's appeal. Charley was more than an Epicurean. To eat and drink, to laugh and talk, and die, was not enough for such a soul. He mentally compared himself to Felix, and said that Vail wouldn't let him forget his duty, anyhow. But for the present it was too delightful to him to honor the entertainment given by the Honorable Mr. So-and-so and Mrs. So-and-so; it was pleasant to be assured by Mrs. Forty-Millions that her party would fail but for his presence. And then he had just achieved the end of his ambition. He was president of the Hasheesh Club. He took his seat at the head of the table on Christmas Eve.

Now, patient reader, we draw near to the time when Charley uttered the exclamation set down at the head of this story. Bear a little longer with my roundabout way of telling. It is Christmastide anyway; why should we hurry ourselves through this happy season?

Just as Charley went into the door of the clubhouse—you remember the Hasheesh clubhouse was in Madison Avenue then—just as Charley entered he met the burly form and genial face of the eminent Dr. Van Doser, who said, "Well, Vanderhuyn, how's your cousin Vail?"

"Is he sick?" asked Charley, struck with a foreboding that made him tremble.

"Sick? Didn't you know? Well, that's just like Vail. He was taken with smallpox two weeks ago, and I wanted to take the risk of penalties and not report his case, but he said if I didn't he would do it himself; that sanitary regulations requiring smallpox patients to go to a hospital were necessary, and that it became one in his position to set a good example to Huckleberry Street. So I was

---

3 The reader will remember that this was written in 1872. I do not know how far the uptown centers of fashion will be in twenty years more.

151

compelled to report him and let him go to the island. And he hasn't let you know?—for fear you would try to communicate with him probably, and thus expose yourself to infection. Extraordinary man, that Vail. I never saw his like," and with that the doctor turned to speak to some gentlemen who had just come in.

And so Charley's Christmas Eve dinner at the Hasheesh Club was spoiled. There are two inconvenient things in this world, a conscience and a tender heart, and Charley Vanderhuyn was plagued with both. While going through with the toasts, his mind was busy with poor Henry Vail suffering in a smallpox hospital. In his graceful response to the sentiment, "The President of the Hasheesh Club," he alluded to the retiring president, and made some witty remark—I forget what—about his being a denizen of Lexington Avenue; but in saying Lexington Avenue he came near slipping into Huckleberry Street, and in fact he did get the first syllable out before he checked himself. He was horrified afterward to think how near he had come, later in the evening, to addressing the company as "Gentlemen of the Smallpox Hospital."

Charley drank more wine and punch than usual. Those who sat near him looked at one another significantly, in a way that implied their belief that Vanderhuyn was too much elated over his election. Little did they know that at that moment the presidency of the famous Hasheesh Club appeared to Charley the veriest bawble in the world. If he had not known how futile would be any attempt to gain an entrance to the smallpox hospital, he would have excused himself and started for the island on the instant.

But it was one o'clock before Charley got away. Out of the brilliantly lighted rooms he walked, stunned with grief, and a little heavy with the wine and punch he had drunk, for in his preoccupation of mind he had forgotten to be as cautious as usual. Following an impulse, he took a car and went directly downtown, and then made his way to Huckleberry Street. He stopped at a saloon door and asked if they could tell him where Mr. Vail's rooms were.

"The blissed man as wint about like a saint? Shore and I can," said the boozy Irishman. "It's right ferninst where yer afther stan'in, up the stairs on the corner of Granefield Coort—over there, bedad."

152

Seeing a light in the rooms indicated by the man, Charley crossed over, passed through a sorrowful-looking crowd at the door, and went up the stairs. He found the negro woman who kept the rooms for Vail standing talking to an Irish woman. Both the women were deeply pitted with smallpox.

He inquired if they could tell him how Mr. Vail was.

"O honey, he's done dead sence three o'clock," said the black woman, sitting down in a chair and beginning to wipe her eyes on her apron. "This Misses Mcgroarty's jist done tole me this minute."

The Irish woman came round in front of Mr. Vanderhuyn and looked inquisitively at him a moment, and then said, "Faix, mister, and is yer name Charley?"

"Why do you ask?" said Vanderhuyn.

"Because I thought, mebbe, you might be after him, the gentleman. It's me husband, Pat Mcgroarty, as is a nurruss in the horsepital, and a good one as iver ye seed, and it's Pat as has been a-tellin' me about that blissed saint of a man, as how in his delairyum he kept a-talkin' to Charley all the time, and Pat said as he seemed to have something on his mind he wanted to say to Charley. An' whin I see yer face, sich a gintleman's face as ye've got, too, I says shure that must be Charley."

"What did he say?" asked Vanderhuyn.

"Shure, and Pat said it wasn't much he could gether, for he was in a awful delairyum, ye know, but he would keep a-sayin', 'Charley, Charley, God and Huckleberry Street want you.' Pat says he'd say it so awful as would make him shiver, that God and Huckleberry Street wanted Charley. Shure it must a bin the delairyum, you know, that made him mix up things loike, and put God and Huckleberry Street together, when its more loike the divil would seem more proper to go with Huckleberry Street, ye know. But if yer name's Charley, and yer loike the loikes of him as is dead, shure Huckleberry Street is after wantin' of you, bad enough."

"My name's Charley, but I'm not a bit like him, though, I'm sorry to say, my good woman. Tell your husband to come and see me — there's my number."

Charley went out, and the men at the door whispered, "That

153

must be the rich man as give him all the money." He took the last car uptown, and he who had been two hours before in that brilliant company at the Hasheesh was now one of ten people riding in a street car. Of his fellow-passengers six were drunken men and two were low women of the town; one of them had no bonnet, and lacked a penny of enough to pay her fare, but the conductor mercifully let her ride, remarking to Vanderhuyn, who stood on the platform, that "the poor devil has a hard life any how." Said I not a minute ago, that the antipodes live not around the world, but around the street corner? Antipodes ride in the same street car.

As the car was passing Mott Street, a passenger, half drunk, came out, turned his haggard face a moment toward the face of Charley Vanderhuyn, and then, with an exclamation of startled recognition, leaped from the car and hurried away in the darkness. It was not till the car had gone three blocks farther that Vanderhuyn guessed, from the golden hair, that this was Perdue, the brilliant "Baron Bertram" of the early days of the Hasheesh Club.

When Charley got back to his luxurious apartment he was possessed with a superstitious feeling. He took up the paper weight that Henry Vail had held in his hand the very last night he was in this parlor, and he thought the whole conversation over as he smoked his cigar, fearing to put out his light.

"Confound the man that invented ghost stories for a Christmas amusement!" he said, as he remembered Old Scrooge and Tiny Tim. "Well, I'm not Old Scrooge, anyhow, if I'm not as good as poor Henry Vail."

I do not know whether it was the reaction from the punch he had drunk, or the sudden shock of Vail's death, or the troubled conscience, or from all three, but when he got into bed he found himself shaking with nervousness.

He had been asleep an hour, perhaps, when he heard a genuine Irish voice say, "Faix, mister, and is yer name Charley?"

He started up—looked around the room. He had made so much concession to his nervous feeling that he had not turned the gas quite out, as was his custom. The dim duskiness made him shudder; he expected to see the Huckleberry Street Irish woman

154

looking at him. But he shook off his terror a little, uttered another malediction on the man that invented Christmas ghost stories, concluded that his illusion must have come from his lying on his left side, turned over, and reflected that by so doing he would relieve his heart and stomach from the weight of his liver, repeated this physiological reflection in a soothing way two or three times, dropped off into a quiet snooze, and almost immediately found himself sitting bolt upright in bed, shaking with a chill terror, sure that the Irish voice had again asked the question, "Faix, mister, and is yer name Charley?" He had a feeling, though his back was toward the table, that some one sat at the table. Charley was no coward, but it took him a minute or two to shake off his terror and regain enough self-control to look around.

For a moment he saw, or thought he saw, a form sitting at the table, then it disappeared, and then, after a good while, Charley got himself composed to sleep again, this time with his head well bolstered, to reduce the circulation in the brain, as he reflected.

He did not get to sleep, however, for before he became unconscious the Irish voice from just above the carved headboard spoke out so clear now that there could be no mistake, "Faix, mister, and is yer name Charley?" It was then that he rose in bed and uttered the exclamation which I set down in the first line of this story. Charley Vanderhuyn could not tell whether he meant Charles Dickens or Nick. Perhaps you can. Indeed, it doesn't seem to matter much, after all.

III

A narrative of this sort, like a French sermon, divides itself into three parts. I have now got through the preliminary tanglements of the history of the founding of the Christmas Club, and I hope to be able to tell the remainder of the story with as few digressions as possible, for at Christmastide a body doesn't want his stories to stretch out to eternity, even if they are ghostly.

Charley Vanderhuyn said "The Dickens!" and though his

meaning was indefinite, he really meant it, whatever it might be. He looked up at the ornamental figure carved on the rich headboard of his bed as if he suspected that the headboard of English walnut had spoken in Irish. He looked at the headboard intently a long time, partly because the Irish voice had come from that direction, and partly because he was afraid to look round toward the table. He knew, just as well before he looked around as he did afterward, what he should see. He saw it before he looked round by some other vision than that of his eyes, and that was what made him shiver so. He knew that the persistent gray eyes were upon him, that they would never move until he looked round. He could feel the look before he saw it.

At last he turned slowly. Sure enough, in that very chair by the table sat the Presence, the Ghost—the—it was Henry Vail; or was it? There, in the dim light, was the aquiline nose like an eagle's beak, there were the steady, unwavering gray eyes, with that same earnest, wistful look fastened on Vanderhuyn; the features were Vail's, but the face was plowed and pitted fearfully as with the smallpox. All this Charley saw, while seeing through the ghost and beyond—the carving on the rosewood dressing case was quite as visible through the unsubstantial apparition as before. Charley was not ordinarily superstitious, and he quickly reasoned that his excited imagination had confounded the features of Harry Vail's face with the pock-marked visage of the Huckleberry Street Irish woman. So he shook himself, rubbed his eyes and looked again. The apparition this time was much more distinct, and it lifted the paper weight, as Henry had three weeks before. Charley was so sure that it was Henry Vail himself that he began to get up to shake hands with his friend, but the perfect transparency of the apparition checked him, and he hid his face in his hands a moment, in a terror that he could no longer conceal from himself.

"What do you want?" he said at last, lifting his eyes.

"I want you, Charley!" said the ghost.

Now I hardly know how to describe to you the manner in which the ghost replied. It was not speech, nor any attempt at speech. You have seen a mesmerist or biologist, or whatever-you-

156

call-him-ist, communicate with a man under his spell without speech. He looks at him, wills that a distinct impression shall be made on his victim, and the poor fellow does or says as the master spirit wishes him. By some such subtle influence the ghost, without the intervention of sound or the sense of hearing, conveyed this reply to Charley. There was no doubt about the reply. It was far more distinct than speech—an impression made directly upon the consciousness.

Charley arose and dressed himself under some sort of fascination. His own will had abdicated; the tender, eager, wistful eyes of Vail held him fast, and he did not feel either inclination or power to resist. The eyes directed him to one article of clothing, and then to another, until he found himself muffled to the ears for a night walk.

"Where are we going?" asked Charley huskily.

"To Huckleberry Street," answered the eyes, without a sound, and in a minute more the two were passing down the silent streets. They met several policemen and private watchmen, but Vanderhuyn observed that no one took notice either of him or the ghost. The feet of the watchmen made a grinding noise in the crisp snow, but Charley was horrified to find that his own tread and that of his companion made no sound whatever as their feet fell upon the icy sidewalks. Was he, then, out of the body also? This silence and this loss of the power of choice made him doubtful, indeed, whether he were dead or alive.

In Huckleberry Street they went first to a large saloon, where a set of roysterers were having a Christmas-Eve spree preparatory to a Christmas-morning headache. Charley could not imagine why the ghost had brought him here, to be smothered with the smell of this villainous tobacco, for to nothing was Charley more sensitive than to the smell of a poor cigar or a cheap pipe. He thought if he should have to stay here long he would like to distribute a box of his best brand among these smokers, so as to give the room the odor of the Hasheesh Club. At first it seemed a Babel of voices; there were men of several different nationalities talking in three or four languages. Six men were standing at the long counter

157

drinking—one German, two Irishmen, a Portuguese sailor, a white American, and a black one. The spirit of Vail seemed to be looking for somebody; it peered round from table to table, where men slammed down the cards so as to make as much noise as possible. Nobody paid the least attention to the two strangers, and at last it flashed upon Vanderhuyn that he and Vail were both invisible to the throng around them.

The Presence stopped in front of a table where two young men sat. They were playing euchre, and they were drinking. It is an old adage that truth is told in wine, and with some men sense comes with whisky.

"I say, Joe," said one, "blamed ef it 'taint too bad; you and me spendin' our time this way! The ole woman's mos' broke 'r heart over me t'day. Sh' said I ought be the s'port 'f her ole dage, 'stid 'f boozin' roun' thish yer way. 'S so! Tell you, Joe, 's so! Blam'd 'f 'taint. Hey? W'at y' say? Hey?"

"Of course 'tis, Ben," growled the other; "we all know that. But what's a feller goin' to do for company? Go on; it's your deal."

"Who kyeers fer th' deal? I d—on't. Now, Joe, I says, t—to th' ole lady, y' see, I says, a young man can't live up a dingy stairs on th' top floor al'ays, and never git no comp'ny. Can't do it. I don't want t' 'rink much, but I c—ome here to git comp'ny. Comp'ny drinks, and I git drunk 'f—fore I know 'fore you—pshaw! deal yerself 'f you want t' play."

After a while he put the cards down again, and began:

"What think I done wunst? He, he! Went to th' Young Men's Chrissen Soshiashen. Ole lady, you know, coaxed. He! he! You bet! Prayer meetin', Bible class, or somethin'. All slick young fellers 'th side whiskers. Talked pious, an' so genteel, you know. I went there fer comp'ny! Didn' go no more. Druther git drunk at the 'free-and-easy' ever' night, by George, 'n to be a slick kind 'f feller 'th side whiskers a lis'nin' t' myself make purty speeches 'n a prayer Bible class meetin' or such, you know. Hey? w'at ye say? Hey? 'S comp'ny a feller wants, and 's comp'ny a feller's got t' have, by cracky! Hey? W'at ye say? Hey, Joe?"

"Blam'd 'f 'tain't," said Joe.

"That's w'at them rich fellers goes to the club fer? Hey? w'at ye say, Joe? Hey?"

"Yes, of course."

"Wish I had a club! Better'n this place to go to. Vail, he used to do a fellow good. If he'd 'a' lived he'd 'a' pulled me out this yer, would, you, know. He got 's eyes onto me, and they say when he got 's eyes onto feller never let go, you know. Done me good. Made me 'shamed. Does feller good t' be 'shamed, Joe. Don't it? Hey? W'at you say?"

"Yes," said Joe.

"But w'en a feller's lonesome, a young feller, I mean, he's got to have company if he has to go down to Davy Jones's, and play seven-up with Ole Nick. Hey, Joe? W'at you say? Hey?"

"I s'pose so," said Joe; "but come, deal, old fellow; don't go to preachin'."

I have heard Charley say that he never heard anything half so distinctly in his life as he felt what the apparition said to him when their eyes met at that moment.

"God and Huckleberry Street want you, Charley."

Charley looked away restively, and then caught the eyes of the ghost again, and this time the ghost said:

"And they're going to have you, too."

I have heard Charley tell of several other visits they made that night; but, as I said before, even a Christmas yarn and a ghost story must not spin itself out, like Banquo's line, to the crack of doom. However true or authentic a story may be—and you can easily verify this by asking any member of the Christmas Club in Huckleberry Street—however true a yarn may be, it must not be so long that it can never be wound up.

The very last of the wretched places they looked in upon was a bare room in a third story. There was a woman sitting on a box in one corner, holding a sick child. A man with golden hair was pacing the floor.

"There's that devil again!" he said, pointing to the blank wall. "Now he's gone. You see, Carrie, I could quit if I had anybody to help me. Oh! I heard to night that Charley Vanderhuyn had been elected president of the Hasheesh. And I saw him an hour ago on a Second Avenue car. I wish Charley would come and talk to me. He'd give me money, but 'tain't money. I could make money if I could let whisky alone. I used to love to hear Charley talk better than to live. I believe it was the ruin of me. But he don't seem to care for a fellow when his clothes get shabby. See there!" and he picked up a piece of wood and threw it at the wall, startling his wife and making the child cry. "I hit him that time! I wish I could hear Charley Vanderhuyn talk once more. His talk is enough to drive devils away any time. Great God, what an awful Christmas this is!"

Charley wanted to begin to talk on the spot, but when he found that poor "Baron Bertram" could neither see him nor hear a word he spoke, he had a fearful sense of being a disembodied spirit. The ghost looked wistfully at him, and said, "God and Huckleberry Street want you, Charley."

Charley was very loath to leave Perdue and his wife in this condition; he would have loved dearly to while away the dreary night for them, but he could not speak to them, and the eyes of the ghost bade him follow, and the two went swiftly back to Charley's rooms again.

Then the apparition sat down by the table and fastened its sad and wistful eyes upon the soul of Charley Vanderhuyn. Not a word did it speak. But the look, the old tender, earnest look of Henry Vail, drew Charley's heart into his eyes and made him weep. There Vail sat, still and wistful, until Charley, roused by all that he had seen, resolved to do what he could for Huckleberry Street. He made no communication of his purpose to the ghost. He meant to keep it close in his own breast. But no sooner had he formed the purpose than a smile—the old familiar smile—came across the face of Vail, the hideous scars of his loathsome disease disappeared, and the face began to shine, while a faint aureole appeared about his head. And Vanderhuyn became conscious that the room was full of other mysterious beings. And to his regret Vail ceased now to regard his friend any more, but looked about him at the Huckleberry Street angels, who seemed to be pulling him away. He and they vanished slowly, and on the wall there shone some faint luminous letters, which Vanderhuyn tried to read, but the light of the Christmas dawn disturbed his vision, and he was able to see only the latter part, and even that was not clear to his eyes, but he partly read and partly remembered the words, "When ye fail on earth they may receive you into everlasting habitations."

He rang for his servant, had the fire replenished, opened his desk and began to write letters. First he resigned the presidency of the Hasheesh Club. Next he begged that Mrs. Rear-Admiral Albatross would excuse him from her Christmas dinner. Unforeseen circumstances, and the death of an intimate friend, were his apologies. Then he sent his regrets, and declined all the invitations to holiday parties. He canceled his engagements to make New-Year's calls[4] in company with Bird, the painter. Then he had breakfast, ordered his carriage, and drove to Huckleberry Street. On the way down he debated what he should do. He couldn't follow in Vail's footsteps. He was not a missionary. He went first and found Perdue, who had been fighting off a threatened attack of tremens all night, relieved the necessities of his family, and took the golden-haired fellow into his carriage. He ordered the coachman to drive the whole length of Huckleberry Street slowly.

"Perdue, what can I do down here? Vail always said that I could do something, if I would try."

"Why, Charley, start a club. That's what these fellows need. How I should like to hear you talk again!"

IV.

How provoking this is! I thought I should get through with three parts. But Christmas is a time when a man can not avoid a tendency to long stories. One can not quite control one's self in a time of mirth, and here my history has grown until I shall have to put on a mansard roof to accommodate it. For in all these three parts I have told you about everything but what my title promised. If you have ever gone through Huckleberry Street—of course you never have gone through such a street except by accident, since you

---

4 The New-Year's call is one of several things alluded to in the text that were in vogue when the story was written, but seem anachronisms in 1893.

are neither poor, vicious, nor benevolent, and only the poor, the vicious, and the benevolent ever go there intentionally—but if you have ever happened to go there of late years, you have seen the Christmas Club building. For on that very morning, with poor "Baron Bertram" in the carriage, Charley resolved to found a club in Huckleberry Street. And what house so good as the one in which Henry Vail had lived?

So he drove up to the house on the corner of Greenfield Court and began to examine it. It was an old-fashioned house; and in its time, when the old families inhabited the downtown streets, it had been an aristocratic mansion. The lower floor was occupied by a butcher's shop, and in the front room, where an old family had once entertained its guests, cheap roasts were being dispensed to the keepers of low boarding houses. The antique fireplace and the ancient mantelpiece were forced to keep company with meat blocks and butchers' cleavers. Above this were Henry Vail's rooms, where the old chambers had been carefully restored; and above these the third story and attic were crowded with tenants. But everywhere the house had traces of its former gentility.

"Good!" said Charley; "Vail preserved his taste for the antique to the last."

"Perdue, what do you think of this for a club-house?"

"Just the thing if you can get it. Ten chances to one it belongs to some saloonkeeper who wouldn't rent it for purposes of civilization."

"Oh, I'll get it! Such men are always susceptible to the influence of money, and I'm sure this is the spot, or Vail wouldn't have chosen it."

And with that Charley and the delighted Perdue drove to the house of Charley's business agent, the same who had been his father's manager.

"Mr. Johnston," said Charley, "I don't like to ask you to work on Christmas, but I want you to find out to-day, if you can, who owns No. 164 Huckleberry Street."

"Do you mean the house Mr. Vail lived in?"

"Yes, that's it. Look it up for me, if you can."

"Oh, that's not hard. The house belongs to you."

"To me! I didn't know I had anything there."

"Yes, that house was your grandfather's, and your mother lived there in her childhood, and your father wouldn't sell it. It brought good rent, and I have never bothered you about it."

"And you let Harry pay me rent?"

"Well, sir, he asked me not to mention to you that he was in your house. He liked to pay his own way. Strange man, that Mr. Vail! I heard from another tenant last night that he is dead."

"Perdue," said Charley, "I wish you would go down there to-day and find out what each tenant in that house will sell his lease for and give possession immediately. Give them a note to Johnston stating the amount, and I want Johnston to give them something over the amount agreed on. I must be on good terms with Huckleberry Street."

Johnston wondered what whim Charley had in his head. "Baron Bertram" completed his negotiations for the leases of the tenants, and then went off and drank Charley's health in so many saloons that he went home entirely drunk, and the next morning was ashamed to see Vanderhuyn. But Charley never even looked a disapproval at him. He had learned from Vail how easy it is for reformers to throw their influence on the wrong side in such a life-and-death struggle as that of Perdue's. In the year that followed he had to forgive him many more than seven times. But Perdue grew stronger in the sunlight of Vanderhuyn's steady friendship.

They had a great time opening the club on New-Year's Eve. There was a banquet, not quite in Delmonico's style, nor quite so fine as those at the Hasheesh; but still it was a grand affair to the dilapidated wrecks that Charley gathered about him. Charley was president, and Vail's portrait hung over the mantelpiece, with this inscription beneath, "The Founder of the Club." Most of Charley's fine paintings were here, and the rooms were indeed brilliant. And if lemonade and root beer and good strong coffee could have made people drunk, there would not have been one sober man there. But Ben delighted "the old lady" by going home sober, owning it was better than the free-and-easy, and his friends all agreed with him.

To Charley, as he looked round on them, this was a far grander moment than when, one week before, he had presided over the gay company at the Hasheesh. Here were good cheer, laughter, funny stories, and a New-Year's Eve worth the having. The gray eyes of the portrait over the antique mantel-piece seemed happy and satisfied.

"Gentlemen," said Charley, "I rise to propose the memory of our founder," and he proceeded to set forth the virtues of Henry Vail. If there had been a reporter present he could have inserted in parenthesis, at several places in Charley's speech, the words, "great applause"; and if he had reported its effect exactly, he would, at several other places, have inserted the words "great sensation," which, in reporter's phrase, expresses any great emotion, especially one which makes an audience weep. In conclusion, Charley lifted his glass of lemonade, and said, "To the memory of Henry Vail, the Founder of the Christmas Club."

"Christmas!" said Baron Bertram, "a good name! For this man," pointing to Charley, "receiveth sinners and eateth with them" (applause).

I have done. Dear friends, a Merry Christmas to you all!

THE END